ILLUMINATION PRESENTS

THE SECRET LIFE OF PeTs2

rhcbooks.com

ISBN 978-1-9848-4991-5 (hardcover)
ISBN 978-1-9848-4992-2 (paperback)
ISBN 978-1-9848-4993-9 (ebook)

Printed in the United States of America

10 9 8 7 6 5 4 3 2 1

ILLUMINATION PRESENTS

THE SECRET LIFE OF

PETs2

Don't laugh.

The Junior Novelization

Adapted by David Lewman

Random House 🏠 New York

CHAPTER ONE

On a beautiful sunny day in New York City, lots of happy kids were playing in Central Park. They ran around chasing each other, hiding behind trees, and screaming with joy and excitement. They were having a great time!

Max, a small brown-and-white dog with a black nose and floppy ears, watched the children curiously. What were they screaming about? Was something wrong? The kids were smiling and laughing, so they seemed happy, but Max didn't get all the screaming. In fact, it made him a little nervous.

Max spotted three kids riding on a large dog's back. He turned to his brother—a big, brown, shaggy dog named Duke—and said, "Ugh. Can you believe that?"

Duke grinned. "Having a kid looks like fun!"

Another dog walked up to them, shaking his head. "Nah, man," he said. "It ain't fun. I'm telling you; once the humans bring home a kid, your life ain't the same."

The large dog with the kids on his back ran right between Max and Duke. They dodged out of the way.

"Seen it a billion times," the dog continued, nodding wisely. "Having a kid changes you."

The next day, Max was walking along the sidewalk with Duke and their owner, Katie. This was one of Max's favorite things to do. He loved it when Katie got out their leashes, snapped them to their collars, and took the dogs outside for a stroll around the bustling city. Just the three of them. No more, no less. And no noisy kids. That was how Max liked it.

A guy on a bicycle noticed Katie walking her dogs. He smiled at her . . . and pedaled right into the back of a parked taxi!

WHAM!

The rider flew over the handlebars and landed on the sidewalk right in front of Katie and her dogs. Luckily, Chuck—that was the bicyclist's name—was wearing a helmet, so he wasn't hurt too badly.

"Are you okay?" Katie asked Chuck, helping him to his feet.

"Oh," Chuck said, looking up at Katie. "Uh, yeah."

Relieved, Katie smiled. Max thought Katie had the best smile in the world. Chuck seemed to like it, too. He smiled back. Duke licked Chuck's face.

SHLURRRP!

"Sorry about that!" Katie said, giggling. "Looks like Duke likes you!"

"That's okay," Chuck said, laughing and wiping the slime off his face. "I love dogs! And their sloppy kisses! Hiya, Duke! How are ya?"

He petted the big hairy dog. Then he reached over and petted Max, too. Max's tail wagged.

Katie smiled, watching the three of them.

Before Max knew it, Katie and Chuck were seeing a lot of each other. Then they got married. And then they were all living together in the same apartment. It was a bit of a change, but Max didn't mind, because he thought Chuck was a good guy. And now Max had two people to throw his ball and take him on walks.

But then, something huge happened . . .

. . . Katie and Chuck had a baby!

"Max, Duke . . . meet Liam!" Katie said when she and Chuck brought their son home from the hospital. Duke and Max walked slowly up to the infant carrier to see the new baby, who was under a blanket. Liam sucked on his pacifier as he smiled at the two curious dogs. Duke smiled back, but Max still wasn't sure how he felt about having a baby in their home. He was pretty sure he was against it.

At first, Liam slept most of the time. Smiling, Katie held him in her arms, rocking back and forth in a rocking chair, humming a lullaby. Max figured Liam was dreaming about . . . whatever babies dream about.

When Max curled up in his doggy bed, Katie and Chuck sat with Liam on the couch, saying things like, "Who's a cute little baby?" and "You, little cutie pie!" Things seemed fine to Max. Liam had his place, and Max had his.

But then Liam started talking. Loudly! When Max was trying to sleep, Liam would screech and wail! He'd stand up in his crib and scream and throw toys! *BONK!* Max had to watch out, or he'd get hit right on the head!

And soon after Liam started making all these loud noises, he started crawling. Sometimes Max would hide in a closet just to get away from him. But if Max dared to peek out of the closet to see if the coast was clear, Liam would come crawling straight at him as fast as he could! Max had to duck back into the closet and hide in its farthest, darkest corner.

Other times, Max tried hiding under the dining

table. But as soon as he settled down for a nice, relaxing nap, Liam would crawl up and bonk him with his ball! This was terrible! Balls were for throwing and fetching, not for bonking dogs on the head! Didn't this baby know that?

Max felt as though his own home wasn't safe anymore. It had been taken over by a little monster! Max tried hiding behind one of the window curtains, but Liam found him and lunged at him, pulling the little dog's tail and yanking at his ears.

Max did his best to keep a safe distance from Liam. But then one day, while Max was lying in his doggy bed, Liam did something Max had never, ever expected. . . .

CHAPTER TWO

Liam crawled right up to the doggy bed and said, "Max!" Then he threw his chubby little arms around Max and hugged him. Max was very surprised! "I love you, Max," Liam said in his little voice. Loved him? Max thought Liam couldn't stand him! Max licked Liam, and Liam laughed.

From then on, everything was different!

Max and Duke became role models for Liam. When they ate dog food out of their bowls, Liam put his bowl of cereal on the floor, got down on his knees, and ate his cereal out of the bowl just like a dog. Liam learned to bury toys in the dirt, too. And when the three of them saw a dog in a book, Liam threw back his head and barked.

Liam did lots of things the two dogs enjoyed, like blowing a hair dryer in their faces. It was just like leaning out of a car window to feel the wind!

When Katie blew bubbles in the apartment, Liam, Max, and Duke had a terrific time chasing them and snapping at them with their teeth. *POP! POP! POP!* "Bubbles!" Liam shouted with delight.

And the best was when Max, Duke, and Liam flopped down on the floor and hugged, Max would think, "I'm still not a kid person. I only like this kid. This is my kid. He's perfect. And I'm never gonna let anything bad happen to him."

Still, there was a tricky side to having Liam around, as far as Max was concerned. Max had always been a fun, happy-go-lucky dog. But once Liam came into his life, Max started to spend all his time worrying about Liam. New York City was a busy place, with millions of people and cars and bicycles and motorcycles and taxis and buses and pigeons and yucky things a kid could pop into his mouth. Max knew it was his job to keep Liam safe.

And his job was turning him into a nervous wreck!

Now when Katie took them for a walk, she slipped a safety harness over Liam's head and held on to a strap. Max thought that putting the baby on a leash was an excellent idea. He and Duke weren't really likely to run away, but with babies, you could never be too careful.

Max spent the whole time watching out for danger. He had to nudge Liam away from dirty wads of gum on park benches and flocks of dangerous pigeons. He could NEVER let his guard down!

One night there was a thunderstorm with lots of loud thunder and flashing lightning. Duke and Liam slept through the storm, but Max was wide awake, trembling, and hearing every *BOOM*. He turned around in his doggy bed, trying different positions, but he just couldn't get comfortable.

Finally, Max jumped onto Liam's bed and lay

down next to him. Half asleep, Liam pulled Max close and murmured, "Good doggy."

That calmed Max down. He smiled, closed his eyes, and fell asleep.

The next morning, the rain had stopped. Drops still dripped off the trees and street signs, but the sun was shining, reflecting off the puddles on the sidewalks.

Chloe, a large gray cat who lived in Max's building, woke up in her living room. Still feeling sleepy, she yawned and stretched.

Then she realized she was hungry. This happened a lot.

Holding her tail high and swaying slightly from side to side, Chloe strolled into her owner's bedroom and hopped onto the bed. Her owner was fast asleep. "Meow," Chloe said lovingly. Her owner kept sleeping. She tried meowing louder. "MEOW." But her owner didn't wake up.

So Chloe batted at her owner's nose. She pushed down on her face with her paws. Still, she slept on.

What would it take to wake this human up? Then Chloe had an idea.

She started hacking up a hairball. That did it. Her owner sat straight up in bed. "Ahhh!" she cried. "No, no, no, no, no, no!"

Chloe paused, ready to spit the hairball on the bed.

"No," her owner warned sternly.

But no one could tell Chloe what to do. She coughed the hairball right onto the clean sheets. *CACK!* And then she smiled.

In the apartment below Max's, a small white rabbit named Snowball slept peacefully in a bassinet in his owner's bedroom. The girl, Molly, was already awake and ready for a new day.

"Good morning, Snowball!" she said brightly. "Who's the best bunny in the whole wide world?" She picked him up and hugged him, burying her face in his smooth, soft, white fur. Snowball acted tough, but secretly he loved when Molly hugged him like that.

Molly carried him into the bathroom, where she brushed her teeth. Then she brushed Snowball's teeth. They glinted and shone in the morning light coming through the window.

While Molly ate her cereal, she and Snowball watched a cartoon on the living room TV. "Take that, evildoer!" cried the superhero in the cartoon. "Off into the sun with you!"

"Yeah!" Molly said as the bad guy got what was coming to him.

The cartoon gave Molly an idea. . . .

CHAPTER THREE

Back in her bedroom, Molly combed Snowball's hair down smooth. Then she said, "Ears up!" The bunny pricked up his ears, and Molly slipped a superhero mask onto his face and hooked it behind his ears. She put a cape on Snowball and set him down on a chair at a small table. Around the table were stuffed animals costumed in superhero capes and helmets. Molly wore a cape, too.

"I'm calling this meeting of the Superhero Animal

Friends to order!" she announced. "Commander Horsey, please read the minutes of the last meeting."

A stuffed horse sat completely still.

"Thank you," Molly said after a moment. "Now remember, everyone, crime is out there! We have to be ready!"

From the living room, Molly's dad called, "Come on, Molly! Time to go!"

Molly looked at the clock on the nightstand next to her bed. "Oh!" she cried. "I'm gonna be late for school!" She whipped off her cape and planted a kiss on top of Snowball's furry white head. "Captain Snowball, you're in charge while I'm gone!" Grabbing her book bag, she hurried out of the room and off to school with her dad.

When she was gone, Snowball took over the meeting. "First of all," he said, "I want to welcome White Thunder back from the washing machine. He was put in there with a red blanket and henceforth will be known as Pink Thunder." Snowball looked at the pink stuffed animal and nodded. "Personally, I like the new look."

The rabbit got up from his chair. "Okay, I'm gonna go check the perimeter." He hopped out of the bedroom and jumped up onto a windowsill. The window was open. Snowball climbed out onto the fire escape and surveyed the metropolis. "Good morning, New York City!" he said, striking a heroic pose.

"Snowball," a voice called. "Hey, Snowball!"

Snowball looked up and saw Max out on his fire escape one floor above, staring down at him. "What are you doing?" Max asked curiously.

"What's it LOOK like I'm doing?" Snowball replied. "I'm looking for crime, Tiny Dog." ("Tiny Dog" was the nickname Snowball had given Max when he first met him, even though Max was actually a lot bigger than Snowball.) "I'm doin' superhero stuff. Let me tell you something: anybody comes in here lookin' for trouble, they're gonna meet my partners." He held up his right front paw. "I'm talkin' about Paw . . ." He held up his left front paw. ". . . and Order!"

"Uh-huh," Max replied, not exactly sure what to make of the new direction the bunny was taking. "Okay, well, you do know that your owner is just playing superhero, right? You're just wearing some superhero pajamas."

Snowball laughed. "Tiny Dog, you are so naive!" He shouted in his best superhero voice, "Point me in the direction of any animal who needs my help . . . and stand back!" He started doing karate moves, kicking with his back paws and chopping the air with his front paws. "HAH! WAH! DEATH BLOW! WUP! JAB! HIIEEEEYAH!"

"Okay, okay," Max said, holding up a paw. "I got it. So did your kid leave for school yet?"

Snowball stopped chopping and nodded. "Yeah, she's got a quiz today. Advanced Spelling. She'll ace it, though. You know, she writes her answers down in ink. That's how confident she is." Snowball thought Molly was the greatest owner ever.

"That sounds really smart," Max admitted. "You know what? Liam is smart, too. In fact, I heard Katie say his head circumference is in the eightieth percentile."

"Oh, that's cool," Snowball said, nodding casually. "That's a lot of head."

"Yeah, it is!" Max agreed enthusiastically. "And also, and this is not exaggerating, Liam knows how to turn on the TV all by himself."

"Nice," Snowball said, secretly thinking that

Max might be a little overly impressed with Liam's skills. "Hey, quick question: Is he still peein' everywhere? Can't control his bladder?"

Max frowned. Was Snowball trying to criticize Liam? "Yeah, he's peeing, but every pet knows if you pee on it, you own it. And Liam is . . . um . . . he's just thinking ahead."

"Yeah, well you still better train 'em before preschool starts. You don't want Liam to get a reputation as one of those pee-pee kids," Snowball said.

Max looked confused. "Preschool?"

"Yeah, he's around that age!" Snowball explained. "The baby bird is leaving the nest, T.D."

"No, no," Max said, shaking his head. "Baby bird is staying put. He doesn't need preschool. He'll stay home with me where it's safe."

Duke poked his big head out of the open window. "Hey, Max. This is no big deal. No need to overreact. But Liam just left."

"WHAT?" Max yelled, freaking out. "Where'd he go?"

"I don't know," Duke said, shrugging his furry shoulders. "They never tell the dog any specifics."

Max rushed back through the open window into the apartment. He headed straight to a basket of dog toys. Digging through them, he quickly found a toy walkie-talkie. Max pressed a button on the walkie-talkie with his paw and said, "This is Home Base to all units! The package has left the building! Does anyone have eyes on him?"

Up on the building's roof, a long black-and-brown dachshund named Buddy peeked over the ledge, watching the front door of the apartment building. "I don't see him," he said into his walkie-talkie. "Over."

In an apartment, Mel, a pug dog who loved to bark at squirrels, was eating a bag of chips. He tapped the button on his walkie-talkie. "He's not in this bag of chips," he reported. "Over."

"Okay," Max answered into his walkie-talkie. "Keep looking for— Wait a minute. Why would he be in a bag of chips?"

Before Mel could explain any further, Norman the guinea pig's voice came over the walkie-talkie. "Home Base, this is Eagle Eye. Don't you worry. I had eyes on the package as soon as he left the building. Over!"

With a walkie-talkie strapped to his head, Norman was driving a remote-control car out on the street, following Chuck and Liam as they walked to an outdoor café. Norman parked his car and stealthily moved in closer as Chuck sat down and offered Liam a cookie shaped like an animal.

"Subject is safe and sound," Norman hissed into his walkie-talkie, "enjoying what looks to be a cookie shaped like a moose. No, wait—it's a reindeer!"

Back in his apartment, Max let out a long breath, relieved by Norman's news. "Okay," he said. "Thanks, Norman!"

CHAPTER FOUR

Max scratched himself intensely with his back paw, working a spot just behind his right ear. He'd been scratching himself a lot lately.

Duke noticed. "Scratching again there, buddy," he pointed out.

Max kept on scratching, ignoring Duke's observation. Muttering to himself, Max said, "I just really don't like it when they take Liam out without me."

Katie entered the room, holding up a rubber ball. "Hey, Duke!" she said in an excited voice. "Ooooo! What's THIS?"

"Oh, I know this!" Duke replied as though Katie could understand him. "It's a ball!"

Katie threw the bouncy ball into the bedroom. "Go get it!"

Duke ran into the bedroom. Katie heard him crash into something as he chased the ball. But instead of going to see what Duke had slammed into, Katie clipped the leash on Max's collar. "Hey, Maxie!" she said. "What say we go for a walk?"

Max wagged his tail happily. He and Katie headed out of the apartment. Out on the sidewalk, Max thought, "I gotta say, this is nice! Good to stretch my legs!"

But as they approached a doorway into a big building, another dog was pulling away from his owner, trying to go in the opposite direction. "I don't wanna go to the vet!" he cried.

"THE VET?" Max said. "No! No, no, no, no, no!" But Katie led Max right to the door of the vet's office and put her hand on the doorknob. "Aww, not cool," Max moaned. "You tricked me."

"Maxie, come on, boy!" Katie pleaded. "You've been so stressed lately, but this vet is gonna help you! Let's go, buddy!" Katie and Chuck had noticed all of Max's scratching and decided to ask the vet for help.

But Max did not want to go to the vet! He dug his claws into the ground, trying to stay outside the dreaded office. Katie had to drag him inside by his leash. She hated to do it, but she knew it was the best thing for Max's health and comfort.

Inside, they crossed the room to a row of seats, and Katie sat down. Huddled by Katie's feet, Max shook with fear. Katie lifted him up onto her lap, trying to calm him.

Max looked around and saw a skinny cat with his owner in the next chair. The skinny cat noticed Max trembling. "First time here?" he asked.

"Uh, yeah," Max admitted.

"Oh, Dr. Francis is the best veterinarian in the business," the cat assured Max. "You're gonna love him. He specializes in behavioral disorders."

Max looked confused. "Behavioral disorders?"

"Yeah," the skinny cat confirmed conspiratorially with a single nod.

"But I don't have a behavioral disorder!" Max protested. "I mean, sure, I worry a little. But it's a dangerous world. You'd be crazy not to worry!"

The skinny cat looked sympathetic. "Yeah, I'm fine, too. It's my human that's nuts. I mean, I bring her a dead bird—she throws it out! I bring her a dead mouse—right in the garbage! IS NOTHING I DO GOOD ENOUGH FOR YOU, MOTHER?" Hissing, the cat swiped at his owner.

"Okay . . . ," Max said slowly, realizing he was talking to a very strange and possibly unwell cat. He looked around the room and saw a hamster running on a wheel.

"I run and I run and I run and I run and I get out, and I've gone nowhere!" the hamster said with a disturbed look in his eye. "NOWHERE!"

Next, Max saw a dog hiding between his owner's legs. He seemed worried. The dog looked up at Max and asked, "My owner always says, 'You're such a good dog,' and I feel like a good dog. But what if deep down I'm a bad dog? What if I'm a *bad* dog?"

Max laughed nervously. "Heh heh." He didn't know what to tell the worried dog. How was Max supposed to know whether the dog was good or bad? He looked around and spotted two adorable kittens. They smiled at him, and he smiled back.

Then they spoke in cute, high-pitched voices. "We start fires!"

Max screamed and fell off Katie's lap. "Max?" Katie asked.

A little while later, Katie and Max returned home. The vet had put a white plastic cone around Max's head to stop him from scratching himself. Max walked into the apartment slowly with his head hung low. Katie leaned over and gently petted his head. Max looked up at her with big sad eyes.

"I know, buddy," she said.

Katie headed into the bedroom, leaving Max alone. He tried to scratch behind his ear, but the cone stopped him. He hated the cone! It smelled weird. It felt uncomfortable. And he was pretty sure it made him look ridiculous.

Searching the room for something to cheer him up, Max spotted his favorite toy under the coffee table. Busy Bee! Just the thing to make him feel better! He'd play with Busy Bee!

Max trotted over to the coffee table and tried to grab Busy Bee in his mouth, but the cone stopped him. *BONK!* He tried going under the table at different spots, but the cone stopped him every time. He tried stretching his front paw to reach the toy. Snatching it with his tongue. Blowing it out from under the table. Reaching for it with his back leg. Tunneling down into the table itself. None of this worked.

From down the hallway, Duke called, "Max! Max!"

Duke barreled into the room and knocked into the coffee table. Max flew off, but once he scrambled to his feet, he saw that Duke had bumped the table away from Busy Bee. He could reach it. Finally!

"You're never going to believe it!" Duke said breathlessly. He noticed Max's new headgear. "Oh, hey, I like your cone." Then he went back to his exciting news. "Listen, I heard Chuck tell Liam that we're going on a trip!"

"Really?" Max asked, thrilled. "We're going in the car?"

"WE'RE GOING IN THE CAR!" Duke replied.

"Car, car, car, car, car, car!" Max chanted.

At the same time, Duke yelled, "Car! Ho ho ho ho ho! Car!"

They grinned at each other.

"Man, you know, life is funny," Max said. "One minute you're getting fitted for a cone, and the next you get to go in the car!"

"I feel like that's very specific to you, but totally, yeah," Duke agreed.

"This is incredible!" Max said. He scooped Busy Bee into his mouth. "I'll be right back!" he managed to say with his mouth full.

CHAPTER
FIVE

Still carrying Busy Bee, Max climbed through the open window onto the fire escape and made his way to Chloe's apartment. He found his friend playing with a springy doorstop. She batted the doorstop with her paw so it made a rattling *THUUUUUNK* sound.

"Chloe?" Max said with his mouth full of his Busy Bee toy.

THUUUUUNK.

He set Busy Bee down. "Chloe, I'm going on a trip, and I—"

THUUUUUNK.

"I was wondering if you'd—"

THUUUUUNK.

Max spoke quickly, trying to slip in his whole request before Chloe hit the doorstop again. "Will you watch my Busy Bee while I'm gone?"

THUUUUUNK. After a moment, Chloe stopped staring at the doorstop and looked at Max, noticing him for the first time. "Oh, hey, Max. Were you saying something?"

"Yeah," Max said. "I was wondering if you could—"

THUUUUUNK. Chloe had gone back to hitting the doorstop.

Max grunted with frustration. "Okay, never mind." He picked up Busy Bee in his mouth and headed back toward the open window he'd come in through.

As he walked away, Chloe asked, "What's that stupid thing on your head?"

Max passed through another window into the apartment where his friend Gidget lived. Gidget was a puffy, little white Pomeranian dog whose owners loved her so much they had several painted portraits of her on their walls. Gidget had a not-so-secret crush on Max.

"Gidget?" Max called. "Gidget, you home? Gidget?"

In the kitchen, Max noticed steam rising from the closed dishwasher. Suddenly, its door dropped open, and he saw Gidget with a towel around her head, taking a nice steam bath. "Oh, hi, Max!" she said, delighted to see him. "You wanna join me?"

"Oh, you know, I really wish I could," Max said. "But, get this . . . I'm going on a trip!"

Gidget's wide eyes opened wider. "Wow! Really?"

"Yeah, it's a big deal," Max explained. "I was wondering . . . could you watch my Busy Bee while I'm gone?"

He showed her the stuffed chew toy. "He is so cute!" Gidget gasped.

"I know," Max agreed. "It's my favorite toy in the whole world. That little face? I mean, come on, look at that little face! Oh, and listen to this!" He tapped Busy Bee with his paw. *SQUEAK!*

Gidget's jaw dropped. "Oh, WOW!" she gushed. "I love him! Oh, I just love him immediately! It's like we're his parents. It's like you're the dad and I'm the mom, and we're in a relationship and this is our baby."

Max looked doubtful. He didn't think it was quite like that. But he really wanted Gidget to take good care of Busy Bee while he was gone. Choosing his words carefully, he said, "Well—"

"It's exactly like that!" Gidget insisted fiercely. "Exactly!"

Max gave in. "Okay, yes, that's exactly what it is. So you'll watch Busy Bee while I'm gone?"

Gidget smiled. "Max, you go. Have a great time. I have got this."

Max smiled a grateful smile. "Thanks, Gidget! See you later!"

He ran out. Gidget stood by the stuffed toy, alert and on guard. "I will defend Busy Bee with my life!" she pledged. Then she gave the bee a little tap with her paw. *SQUEAK!*

"Hee-hee!" she giggled, before going back to her serious guard pose.

Later that day, Chuck drove his and Katie's car down the streets of New York City, heading out of town. Katie sat in the passenger's seat, and Liam was in his car seat. Max and Duke were so excited to be in the car that they couldn't stop climbing all over every inch of it.

From the back seat, Duke stuck his furry head over Chuck's seat, putting his face right next to Chuck's. "Good boy," Chuck told him. But when Duke tried to climb into the front seat, Chuck had to stop him. There wasn't room for the big dog! "Whoa!" Chuck said. "Come on, Duke! You know you don't fit up here!"

Eventually, Max and Duke settled down in the back seat next to Liam. "Yes, yes, yes," Max said happily. "How are we doing, Liam?"

Liam raised both fists in the air. "Woo-hoo!"

"Woo-hoo is RIGHT!" Duke agreed.

Max had an idea. He pawed at the window. "Okay," Katie said, pressing the button to lower the rear window. Max and Duke stuck their heads out, their tongues flapping in the wind.

"Yes!" Max said, forgetting all about the cone he was still wearing.

"Here we go!" Duke added. "Wow!"

Max laughed with joy. Then he took a big sniff. *SNURRRFF!* "You smell that?" he asked.

"Smell what?" Duke asked.

"Everything!" Max answered. "All at once!"

As they sped along, Max noticed a dog sticking his head out the window of the car in the next lane. "Hey, man!" Max called to the other dog.

"I'm in a car!" the dog called back.

"Us too!" Max shouted gleefully.

"I love the car!" the dog yelled.

"It's the best!" Max agreed.

"Ha ha!" The dog laughed. "YES!"

They drove over a bridge, leaving New York City behind. It was the first time Max had ever been outside the city he'd lived in all his life.

CHAPTER SIX

Chuck, Katie, Liam, Max, and Duke drove beyond the city. The dogs kept their heads out the window. They were panting, still excited to be in the car.

A little later, Liam generously shared his juice box with Max and Duke. They were thirsty after riding through the wind with their mouths wide open.

They'd taken care of their thirst, but now they had a different need. . . .

Chuck pulled the car into a rest stop and parked. Katie turned around, facing the toddler and dogs in the back seat. "Okay, come on, guys," she said. "Let's be quick!"

Once they were out of the car, Max and Duke found a tree and lifted their legs. Liam ran over to the tree and lifted his leg, too. But Katie swooped in and scooped him up in her arms before he could do anything. "Oh no, no," she said. "This way, buddy. Come on."

"Nooooooo!" Liam protested. He wanted to be just like his dog pals.

Back in Gidget's apartment, the little dog slept with Busy Bee cradled in her arms by an open window. A soft breeze blew in. She was dreaming a wonderful dream. . . .

Gidget walked with Max down the sidewalk, pushing a fancy baby carriage with Busy Bee lying in it.

They arrived at a beautiful beach, where they lounged on folding chairs, soaking up the sun, listening to the crashing waves of the ocean.

That night, Gidget and Max cuddled on a couch while Busy Bee watched a program on TV. Just as Gidget and Max were about to kiss . . .

SQUEAK!

Gidget hit Busy Bee in her sleep and made the chew toy squeak. The sound woke Gidget up. "Oh no!" she cried as Busy Bee rolled away . . .

. . . and right out the window!

"Oh no, no, no!" Seeing what she'd done, Gidget jumped up and rushed out to the fire escape, watching in horror as Max's beloved toy bounced down the metal stairs. "No, no, no, no!" she shrieked.

She tried to catch Busy Bee in her teeth, but it fell all the way down to a first-floor balcony and bounced through an open window into an apartment. "Gidget," she said to herself accusingly. "What have you done?"

Gidget ran down the stairs of the fire escape to the first-floor balcony. In the window Busy Bee had bounced through, shredded curtains fluttered in the wind.

The little white dog tried to peer past the

curtains into the apartment, but it was too dark inside to see.

She pushed the ragged curtains aside and saw stacks of old newspapers. There was yarn everywhere. An old lady sat in an ancient upholstered chair, watching a game show on TV.

Gidget spotted Busy Bee on the floor near the open window. "Ah!" she said quietly. "Aha!"

She crept through the window into the apartment, a little afraid but determined to retrieve Max's beloved toy. She paused for a moment on the windowsill. The place smelled weird . . . like old fur and canned meat. "Okay," she said, reassuring herself.

But then—*ZWWWIP!*—a paw emerged from under the old lady's chair and grabbed Busy Bee. A cat crawled out from under the chair, holding the stuffed bee.

Then another cat appeared. And another. And another . . .

The apartment was full of cats! They all started fighting over Busy Bee. The old lady didn't seem to mind a bit. In fact, she didn't seem to be aware of what was going on behind her at all. "Hello, pumpkin," was all she said to the tangled ball of fighting cats.

As the cats continued to fight over Busy Bee, one of them glanced toward the open window, thinking he'd heard something there.

It was empty.

Outside, on the fire escape, Gidget was hiding just out of view. Wide-eyed and breathing heavily, she whispered to herself, "Oh, dear sweet Busy Bee!" How was she ever going to rescue Max's favorite toy from all those cats?

Late that afternoon, in Molly's apartment, Snowball was in the living room trying to lift a small pink hand weight. "You know," he grunted, "I'm gonna be the first bunny with washboard abs!"

Chloe was visiting, calmly knocking stuff off shelves and barely listening to Snowball. "Oh, yeah, yeah," she muttered, "that's fascinating."

"Let me tell you something," Snowball said proudly. "Criminals are gonna take one good look at me, and they're just gonna give up!" Straining with all his might, he failed to lift the pink weight. He stopped, breathing hard. "Okay, this is obviously glued to the floor."

A little dog popped her head through an open window. She was wearing a headband with a flower on it. "Excuse me, rabbit, cat," she said politely. "Do any of you know Captain Snowball?"

Snowball looked stunned for a moment. Then he shook himself and stuttered, "Yeah, uh, yeah. Yes. Yes, we do."

"And here we go," Chloe said, rolling her eyes at the thought of things only getting weirder from here.

"Ooo! Good!" the little dog said, coming into the living room. "My name is Daisy, and I really gotta talk to him. A poor, defenseless animal needs saving!"

"Are you saying . . . ?" Snowball asked, amazed that a potential mission had dropped right into his lap so quickly.

"Yes!" Daisy confirmed, with wide-open eyes. "I need Captain Snowball for a"—the little dog leaned in closer and spoke confidentially—"top secret rescue!"

Excited, Snowball turned to go to Molly's bedroom. "All right, well, I gotta go," he said. "But nice meeting you . . . uh . . . What was your name again?"

Daisy looked annoyed. "Okay, you don't listen. It's Daisy."

"Whatever," Snowball said as he hopped down the hallway. "I got to get the dude to get the stuff to do the thing." He looked back over his shoulder. "Bye-bye."

"Mm-hmm," Daisy said, puzzled. "That was weird."

"Oh, sister," Chloe shook her head knowingly. "It's gonna get way weirder."

In Molly's room, Snowball grabbed his superhero costume and pulled it on. "IT'S SNOW TIME, BABY!"

CHAPTER SEVEN

On a city street, a helpless bunny was cornered by three evil villains. "Help!" the little bunny cried.

Suddenly, Captain Snowball landed right between the bunny and the bad guys. "Anybody hungry?" he asked. "HA!" He whipped out two carrots and used them to fight off the bad guys and send them flying. Then he gave a triumphant yell— "AHHHHHH!"—as the third bad guy crashed through a wall.

"Oh, Captain Snowball!" the little bunny said, her heart swelling with love for the brave superhero. He had saved the day.

Captain Snowball struck an action pose and yelled again. "WAAAAAH!"

In the living room, Daisy and Chloe heard Snowball's yell. Chloe rolled her eyes. He was still in the bedroom getting dressed. The whole incident with the helpless bunny and the bad guys had been in his vivid imagination.

Daisy looked toward the bedroom. "Uh, is he okay?"

Chloe was lying on her back. "Not in any way, no."

Wearing his superhero costume, Snowball bounded into the room. "Hello, citizens!" he said in his deepest, most super-heroic voice.

"Who is that?" Daisy asked.

"I'm Captain Snowball!" he explained, putting his fists on his hips. "I hear one of you needs my help!"

Looking excited, Daisy pointed at herself. "Ooo, that's me!"

"Ah, very good," Captain Snowball declared. "New Dog, tell me your story."

Daisy nodded. "Okay, well, it all began when I was on my way back from China, via what some call an *airplane*." She went on to tell her story. . . .

In the cargo storage compartment of an airplane, Daisy and other animals opened their cages and let themselves out. They had a great time playing poker, gambling with the pieces of clothing in the luggage.

Daisy was having fun until she heard a rattling sound and decided to investigate. Searching the darkest corner of the cargo compartment, she found a big cage covered with a tarp that read HAPPY SERGEI'S CIRCUS OF FUN. The whole cage was shaking.

She pulled off the tarp. In the gloom, she could just make out a pair of big, blue, scared eyes. Peering closer, she saw paws in shackles and chains around an animal's neck. She realized it was a young white tiger, chained up and terrified.

In the apartment, Chloe and Snowball listened to Daisy's amazing story. "The tiger's name was Hu!" she said. "The poor baby kitty was being held against his will!"

"Whoa," Snowball said.

"That is unbelievable," Chloe added.

"I know, right?" Snowball agreed.

"No," Chloe clarified. "I mean, I literally don't believe a word of it." She turned to Daisy. "No offense. Or do take offense. I'm good either way."

"Uh, pardon me, offense is very much taken," Daisy said. "That story happened! And it gets WORSE."

When the plane landed in New York City, Daisy was reunited with her owner. As her happy owner was petting her, Daisy saw Hu's cage being loaded into an old, beat-up delivery truck by clowns. Standing next to the truck was Sergei, a mean-looking man in a fur coat.

"Hey, watch it!" Sergei barked to the clowns moving the cage. "Use your no-good clown muscles and push. You clowns are taking too long! Why is it so hard?"

Hu was being taken away to join Sergei's circus. According to Daisy, Sergei was pure, concentrated circus evil!

Having finished her story, Daisy got right to the point. "That tiger needs Captain Snowball!"

Snowball didn't need to hear another word. "Daisy, let's go!"

"Yeah!" Daisy cheered.

Snowball and Daisy ran out of the living room, heading straight through the open window onto the fire escape. "Let's free that tiger!" Snowball cried.

"Or die trying!" Daisy added.

Snowball looked uncertain about that part. "Well," he said, "I mean . . ."

"I mean, we might," Daisy pointed out.

"Um . . . ," Snowball said, still unsure about dying for a tiger he didn't even know.

"Probably you," Daisy said.

Captain Snowball looked startled. "Huh?"

"You're wearing the bright suit," Daisy explained, shrugging. "Everyone's gonna notice you. I'll be fine."

CHAPTER EIGHT

Early that same evening, Max, Duke, and Liam were sleeping peacefully in the car. "Hey, guys!" Chuck said. "We're here!"

"Yay!" Katie cheered.

Max and Duke sat up and looked out the car windows. They saw a beautiful farm with fields, woods, a barn, and a big house with lights gleaming in the windows.

BUH-CAWK!

A chicken fluttered right by the window, startling Max. He drew back.

Katie got out of the car, opened the rear door, and lifted Liam from his car seat. A farmer, who looked like an older, shaggier version of Chuck, stepped off the house's front porch. "Hey there!" he called cheerfully.

"There's Uncle Shep!" Chuck said, grinning.

"Welcome to the farm!" Uncle Shep cried. "Where's my little man?" He held out his arms, and Katie carried Liam over to meet his great-uncle.

Max slowly climbed down from the back seat, careful not to scrape his cone. He'd never been anywhere like this before, and he wasn't sure whether he liked it or not. It was very different from New York City. He could see animals and machines, like tractors, that were different.

"Oh, wow," Duke said enthusiastically as he jumped out of the car. "Look at this place!"

"Yeah," Max said a little nervously. "Yeah, it's—"

"So many smells I have never smelled before!" Duke enthused. "My nose is so confused and happy. Come on, Max, let's go explore." He ran off to sniff around the farm.

51

"Uh . . . wait up," Max said, and took off after his buddy. He found the big shaggy dog greeting a cow grazing on fresh green grass. "Hey, cow!" Duke called to her. "Moooo!"

The cow stared at Duke, chewing her cud.

"You're a cow," Duke said, laughing. "You're supposed to moo!"

"Woof! Woof!" the cow said.

Duke looked surprised. "What?"

"Oh, I'm a dog," the cow said sarcastically. "I'm wagging my tail like an idiot!" She stuck out her tongue and panted like a dog.

"Okay, dude," Duke said, "not cool."

"Oh, are you gonna throw a ball?" the cow continued. "Oh, please throw a ball, and I will chase it because my brain is the size of an acorn!"

Duke frowned. "Okay, yeah, I get it. You've made your point."

But the cow just kept on mocking the dogs. "Oh, look! I'm peeing on a tree! I now own this tree!"

"Okay, great. I'm leaving now," Duke said as he turned away.

"I guess I'll just stare at the door until you come back," the cow called after him.

Max followed Duke. "This place is crazy!" the small dog said.

"Just what you need!" Duke said.

FWUMP! A turkey leg stomped on the ground. The turkey kicked up dirt, revving up, like a bull about to charge.

"What is happening?" Max asked, scared. Through his cone, he saw the turkey running straight at them! "AAAAHHH!" Max screamed as he turned and ran. "No, no, no, no, no!"

The turkey tore after Max. "No, no, no, no, no!" Max kept yelling. He did his best to get away, but the determined turkey was gaining on him.

"DUKE!" Max called. "What did I do? What did I do?"

Max and the turkey ran by a broken-down truck. Inside the truck, a big farm dog named Rooster sat in his special spot, wearing a red bandanna around his neck. He watched the turkey chasing Max, who did not impress Rooster in the slightest. Very few things did.

After a few moments of watching Max run away from the turkey, Rooster leaned out of the truck and let out a single, mighty "WOOF!"

CHAPTER NINE

At the sound of Rooster's bark, the turkey froze in its tracks. All the farm animals stopped what they were doing. When Rooster barked, the animals listened.

"Huh?" Max said, wondering what was going on.

The turkey turned and sulked away, leaving Max alone. Max looked back at the old truck, but Rooster had already lain back down, his work done for the moment.

"Whoa!" Duke said, totally impressed by Rooster's authority. What a dog!

DING-DING! DING-DING!

Uncle Shep was on the porch, ringing the dinner bell. "Dinner's on!" he called.

Duke and Max didn't have to be called twice.

Back in Chloe's apartment, the lights were turned down low and relaxing music played. Gidget crept in through an open window, whispering, "Chloe! I need your help! Chloe!"

Tiptoeing through the apartment, Gidget spotted Chloe sitting on a couch with a lampshade on her head, purring. "Oh," Gidget said, surprised. "Chloe, are you okay?"

"Shhhhhhhh," Chloe hissed like a tire slowly losing air.

"Sorry," Gidget apologized. "Real quick—why is there a lampshade on your head?"

"Heh heh," Chloe chuckled. "Listen, Gidget, baby, I gotta be honest with you. My owner might have given me a little bit of catnip."

Gidget didn't know much about catnip, but she guessed it must make cats feel very relaxed. "Oh, okay, gotcha," she said. "That's great. Um, listen—"

"It is great, Gidget," Chloe interrupted. "Everything isss grrreat."

"All right," Gidget said impatiently. She needed to ask Chloe for help retrieving Busy Bee.

Chloe cocked her head. "Do you hear that?"

"Hear what?" Gidget said, listening.

"It's like a tiny motorrr," Chloe said. "Like a humming sound."

Gidget looked confused. "Tiny motor? Humming? I don't know what you're talking about." Then she realized what the sound was. "Oh, Chloe, you're purring," she said, chuckling. "That sound is you."

"What? That's me?" Chloe asked, surprised. "The sound is coming from inside me?"

"Yep," Gidget assured her.

"Ohhh," Chloe said. "I wonder what other sounds I can make." She giggled and then made a weird sound from deep inside her belly. "MMROWWWER."

Gidget tried to get back to the reason she'd come

to Chloe in the first place. "You see, Max trusted me to look after his Busy Bee, but then——"

"MMRREEEP!" Chloe was trying another sound.

Gidget sighed, exasperated. "Chloe, would you listen?"

"MMRROOOP!"

"Wow," Gidget said, scarcely able to believe Chloe was still trying out weird sounds. "Please stop——"

"MMMRRROP-ABOAP-ADOAP!"

"Are you finished?" Gidget asked, really annoyed.

"MEEP."

Gidget stuck her face close to Chloe's, demanding her attention. "This is important! I lost Busy Bee. I gotta get him back, but to do that . . . Chloe, I need you to teach me"—the little dog dropped her voice to a low conspiratorial whisper—"the way of the cat!"

Back on the farm, the sun was close to setting. Chuck, Katie, and Uncle Shep were eating dinner at a big picnic table in the front yard. Uncle Shep had put out all kinds of delicious food, fresh from the farm. Liam was playing in a portable playpen with Max standing guard nearby. He was convinced that the farm presented all sorts of new dangers to Liam, and he wanted to be ready. He kept looking back and forth, swinging his plastic cone from side to side.

Duke was jumping around trying to catch fireflies. "Here we go! I'm gonna getcha!" he told the fireflies joyfully. "Max, come on! Try to catch a firefly!"

"That sounds great, but I think Liam wants me near him," Max said. "You know, he's a little freaked out being in this weird place."

Duke looked at Liam. He was playing with his toys, looking completely happy and not at all freaked out. "I think he'll be okay," Duke suggested.

"Okay," Max said hesitatingly. "Just one firefly."

Max jumped up and snapped with his mouth. "Yes! I . . . UGH! AAAAUGH!" He stuck out his tongue. It had glowing green firefly goop on it. Looking around desperately, Max spotted a water bowl on the ground and ran over to it. He started lapping up water.

Rooster shoved his face right in front of Max's. "Ahh!" Max yelled, startled. Then he recognized the big dog who'd stopped the turkey for him. "Oh. Hello."

"A dog's got two things in this life," Rooster growled. "His water bowl and his dignity. You take one, you take the other."

"I, uh, didn't know this was your bowl," Max said.

"That cone blocking your view?" Rooster asked. "The bowl's got my name on the side."

Rooster spun the bowl around. On the other side was a picture of a rooster.

"We are so sorry, Mr. Chicken," Duke said.

Rooster glared at Duke. "Name's not *Chicken*!" he snarled. "Do I look like a chicken to you?"

"No," Max said, cringing. "No, sir."

"No," Duke agreed. "Not even a little bit."

"Name's Rooster," the big dog told them.

"Oh, okay," Max said. "I'm Max, and this is—"

"Hey, what's that kid doing in the cage?" Rooster

interrupted, nodding his head toward Liam. "Something wrong? He got the fever?"

"That's Liam," Max explained. "He likes to run."

Rooster shrugged. "So let him run."

Max gave a knowing look. "Well, Liam's superfast. We blink, and he's up a tree."

"So then your kid's up a tree," Rooster said in his low, raspy voice. "What's the problem?"

To Max, the problem seemed incredibly obvious. But this farm dog didn't quite understand. "Well . . . ," Max said slowly and clearly, "he could fall."

"He might," Rooster agreed.

Rooster still didn't seem to get it. "And then he hurts himself," Max explained.

"Oh, so he got really high up in this hypothetical tree," Rooster said sarcastically.

"I . . . nungh . . ." Max made a frustrated sound. It seemed to be impossible to explain the perils that Liam faced to Rooster.

"Kid gets hurt, he learns not to do it again," Rooster said. "You know how many electric cords I've chewed?"

Max had no idea. "Like, multiple cords?"

"One," Rooster said. "It shocked me. I walked backward for a week. But I never chewed a cord again."

Max shook his head. "That is great for you—and it, um, explains a lot—but I like to protect Liam from everything."

Rooster was already walking away. "Well, that's you. And you're wrong."

CHAPTER TEN

Max was mad at Rooster for saying he was wrong. He turned to Duke. "Can you believe that guy?" he demanded.

"Yeah, he was cool," Duke said enthusiastically.

"No! He wasn't!" Max snapped.

"I know!" Duke agreed, wanting to be on his friend's side. "He wasn't cool at all."

Uncle Shep and Katie cleared dishes off the

picnic table and carried them inside. Chuck lifted Liam out of his playpen and carried him into the house. It was starting to get dark.

"Come on," Duke said to Max. They trotted up onto the porch and started to walk through the front door.

"Whoa," Uncle Shep said in his friendly voice. "Hold up there. Dogs sleep outside."

"Uh, pardon?" Max said.

"Huh?" Duke said. The two of them always slept inside the apartment with Katie, Chuck, and Liam. Now they were supposed to spend the night out in the dark?

"Whoa, whoa, whoa, whoa," Max said. "Wait. Let's talk about this like rational—"

SLAM! The front door closed.

"Oh," Max said, stunned.

Pedaling a pink plastic tricycle with one big wheel in front and two little ones in back, Captain Snowball pulled onto the grounds of a circus. He climbed off the tricycle and checked his pulse while trying to catch his breath. He'd been pedaling hard. Daisy got off the back of the tricycle.

"All right," Snowball gasped. "We're here. In record time, too, thanks to the Bunnymobile."

"Oh yeah!" Daisy agreed.

Snowball spotted a nearby cardboard box, dragged it over to the tricycle, and covered the Bunnymobile with the box. "Stealth mode," he explained. "Let's go!"

As Daisy trotted quietly under a banner that read HAPPY SERGEI'S CIRCUS OF FUN, Snowball stuck to the shadows, rolling and hopping, bouncing and banging into things and generally not being very stealthy at all. Making their way through the circus, they looked for clues as to where Hu the white tiger was being kept. When Snowball turned a corner, he found himself face to face with a big scary clown!

"AAAAAH!" Snowball screamed. Looking closer, he realized the clown was just a clown-shaped trash can.

"You are jumpy," Daisy observed.

Snowball tried to appear calm. "I mean 'Aaaaah,

that's cool!' Or 'Aaaaah, look at that thing I'm not scared of right there.'" He pointed at a piece of trash on the ground. "Or 'Aaaaah, there's a candy wrapper on the ground.' See? It's just a thing I do."

Nearby, Sergei growled, "Come on, you stupid tiger!" *CRACK!*

Daisy and Snowball heard a whip, followed by the whimpers of a scared cat.

"There he is!" Daisy whispered. "Let's go!"

The two rescuers snuck into a circus tent and hid underneath the bleachers. Sergei snarled, "We don't have all night!"

When Snowball and Daisy peeked out from underneath the bleachers, they saw Hu perched nervously on a high platform next to Sergei. On the ground below the platform was a tiny pool of water.

"You're wasting Sergei's time!" the evil circus owner barked. He held up a long leather whip. He snapped it. Terrified of the sound, Hu shrank back.

Horrified, Daisy whispered to Snowball, "We gotta do something!"

SPLASH! Hu fell into the tiny pool of water!

"Come on!" Captain Snowball said.

A little while later, Hu was locked in his cage just outside the tent. Five wolves guarded the cage. They had chains around their necks that were attached to stakes in the ground.

"We try again tomorrow," Sergei warned. "If tiger does not do trick, then Sergei turns tiger into rug!" He looked at the wolves. "Do not let tiger out of your sight." He hung a ring of keys on a hook and stomped away.

Hu cowered in his cage. Snowball and Daisy ran over to him. "It's okay, Hu," Daisy reassured him. "It's me, Daisy. From the plane."

The tiger's eyes went wide in surprise. He nuzzled Daisy through the bars. He was happy to see her.

"HEY!" snapped one of the wolves. "Step away from the tiger!"

"MIND YOUR BUSINESS, WOLF!" Daisy snapped back. The rest of the wolves perked up, ready to take on this little dog.

Daisy spotted the ring of keys on the hook, just past the wolves. "Ooooo," she said, excited to see the very thing she needed to let Hu out of his cage. She started running between the wolves, heading for the keys. She jumped up onto the wolves' backs, leaping from wolf to wolf as they wheeled and snapped at her. Their chains started to tangle up.

Hoping to smash the lock on Hu's cage, Snowball picked up a large mallet. But it was far too heavy for him to lift. He fell backward. "AAAAAH!"

One of the wolves strained and pulled at his chain until the stake ripped out of the ground. "Huh?" Snowball said when he saw the wolf pull free. "AAAAAHHH!" He took off. The wolf chased after him, dragging his chain and stake behind him.

The four other wolves kept snapping at Daisy, but she managed to dodge their long, sharp fangs. "Ha ha!" she laughed triumphantly. But she still couldn't quite reach the ring of keys. The hook was just beyond her grasp.

The wolf who had broken free chased Snowball through carnival game booths until Snowball froze among plush prizes, pretending to be a stuffed animal. He thought he was in the clear until—

SNAP! The wolf reappeared, snapping his jaws!

Snowball leapt away just in time, feeling the wolf's hot breath on his fur. He grabbed a water gun from one of the booths and squirted the wolf in the face. Then he started running, with the wet wolf in hot pursuit.

As he sprinted through the circus grounds, Snowball nervously chanted to himself, "Gonna die, gonna die, gonna die . . ."

CHAPTER ELEVEN

Snowball ran as fast as he could, zigzagging over the seats of a carnival ride. The wolf chasing him leapt through the air with his mouth open and his white teeth shining. Snowball clenched his eyes shut tight, waiting for the wolf's attack—but the wolf's chain snagged on one of the ride's cars! He was stuck! A safety bar lowered over the wolf, holding him in the car. Someone had pressed a button in the control booth, lowering the metal bar. A paw pressed another button, and the ride started up. The wolf was whisked away on the carnival ride!

Snowball opened his eyes and saw Daisy in the booth. She was controlling the ride! "Huh?" he said, surprised to see her there. She was holding a ring of keys in her mouth. "I goff duh keez!" she said with her mouth full. "Leff cho!"

"What?" Snowball asked, unable to understand what she was saying.

Daisy spat out the key ring, hit a button with her paw, and spoke into a microphone. Her voice came out through a loudspeaker. "I SAID I GOT THE KEYS! COME ON! LET'S GO!"

She ran out of the booth. "All right," Snowball said, following her. "Yeah, of course."

They quickly made their way to Hu's cage and used the keys to swing the door open. Hu smiled, happy to see his friend Daisy. She and Snowball bumped paws and said, "Boom!" They hurried away with the tiger, passing the guard wolves, still tangled in their chains.

"You know what I learned today?" Daisy said. "Wolves are jerks."

Bound together, the wolves growled.

Meanwhile, out in the country, Duke was sound asleep on the front porch of the big farmhouse. Max was wide awake, worrying about Liam. "Duke," he whispered. "Psst. Duke! I think we should check on Liam." He waited a moment for his brother to answer. "Duke!"

But Duke just mumbled in his sleep, "I finally caught you, tail."

Unable to wake Duke, Max headed off all on his own into the dark. He carefully stepped off the porch into the wet grass and started walking around the house. He peered in a window. No Liam. He moved to the next window and looked in. There he was! Liam was fast asleep, smiling and happy.

Max smiled, too. If Liam was happy, he was happy, though he longed to be inside the house with him. He headed back toward the front porch.

CHIRP! CHIRP!

"What's that?" Max hissed, alarmed. He looked around and spotted a small bird.

SQUAWK!

He froze. Max saw a much larger crow on a branch. "Okay, okay . . . ," he said, trying to calm himself down. He started to take a step, but—

CROAK! SCREECH!

"What?" he said. He tried to see what was making these sounds in the night, but the cone made it tricky. All of a sudden, the night sounds came at him thick and fast! A raccoon snarled. A deer grunted. A cricket chirped. Duke snored. A squirrel gnawed on corn. A turkey gobbled. A cow farted. A coyote howled. *AROOOO!*

"AHHH!" Max yelled. He'd thought the city was noisy, but it seemed like nothing compared to the farm at night.

Then Max got a creepy feeling, like something was watching him. He looked at the bushes behind him. Something was moving in there! He took a couple of steps forward, then looked back behind him again. Nothing. He swiveled his cone forward and saw . . . A FOX! RIGHT IN HIS PATH!

"Aaaaah! Wait, wait, wait, no! Please!" Max begged the creature. "You don't want to eat me! I'm skin and bones!"

The fox moved toward him. Max backed away. "No, no, no, no, no," he repeated.

The fox crouched down, ready to pounce. Max closed his eyes. "So this is how it ends?" he thought, his four legs trembling.

WOOF! With a mighty bark, Rooster charged out of the darkness straight at the fox, chasing it through the thick grass! The fox ran away through the moonlight.

Rooster trotted back, spat out a tuft of fox hair, and shot Max a cold, annoyed look.

"Uh, thanks," Max said, laughing nervously. "He got the jump on me. I guess I couldn't see him because of the cone."

Rooster shrugged. "Then get rid of the cone."

Max looked puzzled. "What was that?"

"Ditch it," Rooster said.

"Oh man, I would," Max claimed. "I would, but my therapist says I need it."

Rooster made a face like something smelled bad. "Oh, okay. Well, that makes sense." That was what Rooster said, but he thought that what Max had said made absolutely no sense at all.

Max bought it. "Yeah," he said, chuckling. "It's a medical device. These doctors—"

Suddenly, Rooster lunged at Max! "AAAAH!" Max screamed.

Rooster ripped the cone off Max's head with his teeth and tossed it to the ground. "There," he said. "You're cured. Hallelujah." He walked away, smiling.

Max watched Rooster go, stunned that he'd just ripped the cone off without even asking.

"Not a fan," Max grumbled to himself. "I am not a fan of the farm."

In her apartment, Chloe slipped a sock over Gidget's tail, saying, "Tail . . ." She placed cat ears on the little dog's head. "Ears . . ."

Wearing her new tail and ears, Gidget stood still. Mel, Buddy, and Sweetpea, a little green budgie bird with a yellow head, checked out her new feline look.

"Whoa!" Mel exclaimed with his usual gusto. "Gidget, you look so much like a cat, it's crazy!"

"Yeah!" Gidget said, pleased. "Who knew? So easy!"

Chloe held up her paw. "Hold on," she said. "That's not all. Now you gotta learn how to act like a cat."

"Okay," Gidget agreed, nodding. Her cat ears slipped a little. She straightened them.

Chloe paced back and forth like a drill sergeant in front of a line of soldiers. "I'm gonna throw some situations at you," she said sternly. "Gidget, you react like a cat."

"Gotcha," Gidget said confidently.

Chloe batted a ball with her paw, sending it rolling across the floor. "FETCH!"

"YES!" Mel cried.

"I'm gonna get it!" Buddy exclaimed, skittering across the floor after the ball.

Gidget was very excited, shifting from paw to paw, eager to chase after the ball. But Chloe stopped her from running. Gidget was practically bursting with anticipation. She could almost taste the ball in her mouth.

"Gidget, stay," Chloe commanded.

"But—" She was dying to chase that ball.

"No!" Chloe barked. "Cats don't care about fetching. Fetching is for dopes!"

Mel was happily sprinting after the ball, chasing under chairs and sofas.

"You're above that," Chloe explained to Gidget. "You're a cat."

"Right," Gidget said, watching Mel and Buddy playing with the ball, and letting go of the urge to chase it. "I'm a cat."

Moments later, Gidget, Mel, and Buddy were lined up on a shelf. Chloe walked behind them and shoved Mel and Buddy off.

"Aaaah!" Mel cried.

"Why?" Buddy yelled.

THUD! They both landed awkwardly on the floor below in a little heap.

"See? Dogs land like the clumsy oafs they are," Chloe explained. "Cats land on their feet."

"Really?" Gidget wondered. "How do they do—"

Chloe shoved Gidget off the shelf.

"AAAAH!" Gidget yelled, falling through the air. But somehow, she landed on her feet! "Yes!" she cheered. "I did it! I landed on my feet! Yes!"

Mel and Buddy, still sprawled on the floor, wagged their tails in appreciation. "Nice work!" Buddy complimented Gidget.

"Ow," Mel said.

Next, Chloe led Gidget, Buddy, and Mel to her litter box. Mel jumped in and started digging right away. Chloe gestured toward the litter box, inviting Gidget to use it. "You gotta. It's a fact of life."

"Absolutely not," Gidget responded. "Never gonna happen."

Mel looked up from his digging. "Guys! I found treats!"

"Aww, Mel," Buddy said sadly, shaking his head.

For Gidget's next cat lesson, Chloe placed her next to Sweetpea. "Okay, Gidget," Chloe said. "Eat Sweetpea."

Gidget looked appalled. "What?"

"Cats eat birds," Chloe explained, shrugging. "It's nature."

"Yeah, I'm gonna pass," Gidget said.

Chloe shook her head. "No, no, no, no. You used your one pass on the litter box, so you have to do this."

"But . . ."

"But-but-but-but-but—DO IT!" Chloe ordered.

CHAPTER TWELVE

Buddy leaned in close to Chloe. "You're seriously gonna make Gidget eat Sweetpea?" he asked.

Chloe turned to the dachshund and whispered, "Oh no, no, no. Of course not. I'm just freaking her out."

"Okay," Gidget said with her mouth full. A single green feather floated out from between her lips. Her cheeks were full of Sweetpea. "What's next?"

"Gidget, NO!" Chloe said sharply. She couldn't believe Gidget had actually eaten Sweetpea. "Bad dog! Bad cat-dog!"

Gidget opened her mouth, and Sweetpea flew out unharmed. The little bird gave Gidget an angry peck.

"Blaaaaaah," Gidget said, spitting out feathers. "Sorry." But Sweetpea was in no mood to hear the apology.

Gidget's final test was to bother a human working on a computer. In this case, the "human" was made out of pillows, sunglasses, and a hat. It was propped up at a desk as though it were using a laptop. Chloe sat nearby on a windowsill while Mel and Buddy watched.

"Up!" Chloe commanded. Gidget jumped onto the desk with some difficulty—it was pretty high for a little Pomeranian pretending to be a cat.

"And . . . tail in the face!" Chloe ordered. Gidget walked on the desk and stuck her tail right in the fake human's face.

"Okay, touch the butt to the coffee cup," Chloe said. Gidget planted her butt right on the fake human's coffee cup.

"Walk on keyboard," Chloe directed. Following directions perfectly, Gidget walked right across the laptop's keyboard.

"There you go!" Chloe said approvingly. "Coffee on computer!" Gidget kicked over the cup of coffee, spilling it right on the computer.

"And down!" Chloe said. Gidget jumped down off the desk, her destructive work done.

"Nice," Buddy said.

Even Chloe was excited for once. "Yes! You got it!" she cried. "Gidget, you're as close to *cat* as a dog can get!"

Gidget smiled and her eyes sparkled with determination: she was ready to rescue Busy Bee.

"Cool! Now turn me into a chinchilla!" Mel said.

Captain Snowball strutted down a dark New York City street, very proud of rescuing Hu from Sergei's evil circus. Daisy walked beside him. "Oh yeah!" Snowball crowed. "First mission in the bag! It was easy. Too easy? Maybe. Maybe it was."

The tiger was springing from roofs and hoods of

parked cars, having a great time.

Snowball turned to a passing stray dog. "Hey, big fella! What'd I just do? Oh, I rescued a tiger! I'm not even trying to brag. I'm just telling you what happened. See, that's the thing about being awesome. When you're awesome and you just tell the truth, it sounds like you're bragging. But you're not! Not at all! You're telling the AWESOME TRUTH ABOUT YOUR AWESOMENESS!"

Daisy rolled her eyes. "Let me know when you finish tooting your horn, 'cause we gotta find a safe place for Hu."

Snowball was so caught up in playing superhero that he'd almost forgotten about the tiger for a second. "Uh, what?" he said. "What are you talking about?"

Daisy pointed. Snowball saw Hu playfully swat the bumper off a car. "Oh yeah," Snowball said. "Oh, that guy. Yeah." He thought for a moment. "Oh! I got it! I know a guy whose owner is never home! Yeah, we can take Hu there!"

"Sounds like a plan!" Daisy said, smiling.

"Super bunny powers ACTIVATE!" Captain Snowball cried, running off.

Early the next morning, Snowball, Daisy, and Hu climbed a fire escape to a window in the apartment where Pops lived. Pops was an old basset hound. His back legs didn't work anymore, so he used a cloth sling connected to two wheels as a cart to get around. But that didn't stop him from going all over New York City if he had a good reason to.

The bunny, the dog, and the tiger paused outside the window. "Wait out here," Snowball told Hu. Then he turned to Daisy and said, "Now, you let me do all the talking." He put a big friendly smile on his face and headed inside.

Pops was addressing a bunch of puppies and one kitten. "I'm a puppy cute and sweet," he chanted. "Beg real nice and get a treat! Hep! Hep! Hep!"

Snowball greeted the old dog. "Hey, Pops."

Pops raised his head, looking puzzled. "Who . . . who's that?" He and the puppies turned and saw Snowball.

"Bunny! Bunny!" the puppies all said, excited. They ran straight toward him.

"Oh, uh . . . . AHHHH!" Snowball yelled as the puppies swarmed all over him. "I am a hero! I need you to respect that!"

"All right, all right," Pops wheezed. "TEN HUT!" The puppies scrambled off Snowball and lined up like soldiers. "Puppy School is in session," the old hound announced.

"Puppy School?" Snowball asked. He'd never heard of a school for puppies.

"Now the daily pledge!" Pops told the puppies. "I promise . . ."

"I promise . . . ," echoed the puppies in unison.

". . . to listen to Pops . . . ," Pops said.

". . . to listen to Pops . . . ," the puppies repeated.

". . . and learn how to be adorable, wide-eyed, and loving . . ."

". . . and learn how to be adorable, wide-eyed, and loving . . ."

". . . to get what I want, when I want it!"

". . . to get what I want, when I want it!"

"Okay!" Pops said. "Now Pops's Quiz!" He nodded toward his assistant, a hamster named Myron. "Myron has hidden socks all over the room. Now, what do we do with human socks?"

A tiny puppy named Princess stepped forward, eager to be called on. "Oh, me! Me!"

Pops smiled at her. "Go ahead, Princess."

"We hide 'em, Mr. Pops," she said confidently.

"Correctaroonie!" Pops said, nodding approvingly. "And why do we hide them?"

Princess sounded as if she was repeating something Pops had told the puppies many times. "Not knowing where one sock is messes with the humans' minds."

"Heck, yes it does!" Pops said, wheezing with laughter. "Always keep 'em guessing! Now go find those socks." The puppies scattered, searching the room for the socks Myron had hidden.

But instead of searching for socks, a puppy named Tiny was licking Snowball. "Whoa! Okay, all right," Snowball said to Tiny. He called to Pops. "Hey, Pops! What's—" The bunny looked down at Tiny. "Okay, that's enough! Hey!" Then he looked up and spoke to Pops again. "What's going on?"

"My owner got a new puppy," Pops explained, pointing to Tiny, who looked like a miniature Pops.

"My name's Tiny!" the puppy announced.

"I was teaching Tiny how to not be anyone's

sucker," Pops said. "Word got out, and suddenly every puppy in the tristate area was scratching at my door." A chubby puppy named Pickles ran up to him. "Professor Pops?" he asked.

"Yes, Pickles?" Pops said.

"I gotta make a poop!"

"Oh, you know where to do that," Pops said, chuckling. "Find a shoe!"

Daisy watched Pops teaching all the puppies and smiled. "This is so sweet."

"Yeah, they're good pup—" Pops started to say. But just then he looked up and saw Hu gnawing on the couch. "Holy cheese and crackers!" he shouted. "WHAT IS THAT?"

CHAPTER THIRTEEN

"Myron! Horn!" Pops ordered. The helpful hamster blew a loud air horn. *BLAAAT!* Hu leapt straight up in the air and dug his claws into the ceiling. He hung there, upside down.

"No, no, no!" Snowball cried. "Look, it's okay! This beautiful creature is Hu! And the good news is, he's staying with you."

CRASH! Hu fell from the ceiling, bringing big chunks of plaster with him. "Get that tiger out of here before he does any more damage!" Pops insisted.

"But we don't have anywhere else to take him!" Snowball pleaded.

Pops put on his most stubborn face. "Well, he ain't staying here!"

Suddenly, all the puppies pounced on Hu. The tiger loved it! "Kitty! Kitty! Kitty! Kitty!" the puppies squeaked.

Pops couldn't believe what he was seeing. "What are you doing? Don't get attached! That thing is out of here!"

"Awwww," said the puppies, super disappointed.

Pickles walked by. "Oh, Pickles," Pops said, "did you poop in a shoe?"

"I pooped in a boot!" Pickles said proudly. "Your owner won't find it for weeks!" Pops tightened his mouth and sniffed.

"Are you crying?" Daisy asked him.

"What? No! YOU'RE crying!" Pops said, trying to hide his emotion. "But I'm just so proud of Pickles."

The puppies surrounded Hu with big sad eyes and started whining. "Mr. Pops," Princess begged, "please can the tiger stay with us? Please?"

"PLEASE?" begged all the puppies, making their eyes even bigger. Hu made his eyes big, too, looking at Pops pleadingly.

"Oh, flapdoodle," Pops said, giving in. "Okay, fine—one night."

"YAY!" all the puppies cheered. "WOO-HOO!"

Pops shook his head. "I taught you guys too well."

That morning, Sergei stomped past his wolves and stared at Hu's empty cage. He was furious. "I give wolves one job—guard white tiger! And you wolves, you blow it! Maybe I should make juggling monkey head of security! What say you, Little Sergei?"

A monkey, Little Sergei, sat on his shoulder. The monkey smiled and clapped his hands, liking the idea of being head of security.

"Yes, you are so smart!" Sergei said to his monkey.

Two circus workers carried in the wolf trapped in the carnival ride. Sergei sneered at the wolf, disgusted. "And then there's this one!" he said. "You're the worst wolf ever. I swear I—"

One of the wolves was sniffing something on the ground. Sergei picked it up. It was the flower from Daisy's headband. "What's this?" Sergei said, smelling the flower. "This is from thief of tiger?"

He offered the flower to the wolves. "Yes, smell!"

The wolves went wild, sniffing and snarling. Sergei removed their collars from the chains holding them. "You bring that tiger back!" he commanded. The wolves circled around Sergei, who pointed at the wolf stuck in the ride. "And if you don't, that one will be a new coat for Little Sergei!"

He stomped away, and the wolves tore off down the street, howling. *HOWR-ROOOO!*

At the same time that morning, Duke was eating from a bowl near the front porch of the farmhouse. Nearby, Max was watching Liam. "Mmm, this is good," Duke said, chewing. "You should really try this. Mmm!"

Clutching a book in his hand, Liam looked at Max and said, "Max, book, book, book!"

"Oh, sorry, Liam," Duke apologized. "We can't read."

Max trotted over to look at the book. "Well, wait a second," he told Duke. "There's no reason we can't figure this out together, right?"

Liam opened the book to the first page. "There's a little girl in a red hood skipping through the forest with some food," Max said. "Look at that! She's got food!"

"Om nom nom!" Liam said, pretending to eat an imaginary snack. He turned the page. A lovely drawing showed the little girl approaching a bed. Someone was in the bed, but the person's face was in shadow.

"And look at that!" Max said cheerfully. "She brought the food over to . . . oh, say, who is that?"

"Looks like her grandma!" Duke suggested.

"I bet you're right!" Max agreed. "Aww, that is sweet. She—"

Liam turned the page. The person in the bed was clearly a big bad wolf.

"Ohhhhh," Duke said.

"Ahhhhh!" Max yelled.

"Ummm?" Liam said, confused.

"Uh, right," Max said, trying to come up with an explanation of the picture that wasn't scary. "So, Grandma had a pet wolf. They had a great visit, the little girl went home, and no one got eaten. The end." He gave a nervous little laugh.

Rooster walked up. He'd heard what Max said. "No, no, no," he said. "That's not how the story goes."

Max shot Rooster a look. "We got this, thanks."

Rooster ignored him. "That wolf is going to eat the little girl."

"Nope!" Max said. "Thank you, Rooster."

"He already ate Grandma," Rooster continued, "and then he assumed the old lady's identity."

"Noooooo!" Liam howled.

CHAPTER FOURTEEN

"Don't freak out my kid!" Max scolded Rooster. But Liam didn't really seem freaked out. He was smacking his hand against the picture of the wolf in the book. *WHAP! WHAP! WHAP!* "Take that, Mr. Wolfy!" he said sternly.

"Kid seems fine to me," Rooster said, heading off. "You're the one who's scared of everything."

Max frowned. "I am not! I'm . . . I'm . . . tell him, Duke!"

"Yeah, Max isn't scared of everything," Duke called to Rooster. "I can think of, um . . ." He paused, thinking hard. "Um, yeah, well, there's a few things . . ." He tried, but off the top of his shaggy head, Duke just couldn't think of anything Max wasn't afraid of.

"Okay, thanks," Max sighed.

"You bet!" Duke said brightly.

That same morning, Gidget stood on the fire escape outside the old cat lady's apartment with Norman the guinea pig. She wore her cat disguise. "Okay, Norman, this is it. You're good to go?"

"Roger that," Norman said, giving a little salute in the affirmative. He ran up the side of the building while Gidget headed to the window. She took a deep breath and crept through, into the apartment. When the other cats noticed her, they moved forward, unsure of exactly what the new creature was. Suddenly, the old lady stepped between them and Gidget. She patted Gidget on the head and said, "That's a good kitty."

"Meow," Gidget replied coolly in her best cat voice. Then she turned and hissed at the other cats, daring them to come near her.

That was good enough for the cats. They quickly lost interest in Gidget. She was apparently just another cat.

As Gidget walked by a cat scratching the old lady's chair with its claws, she heard a familiar sound above her head. *SQUEAK! SQUEAK!* She looked up and spotted Busy Bee on top of a carpeted cat tower. "Busy Bee!" she whispered to herself.

Gidget started to climb. But when she reached the top of the tower, she saw a gigantic sleeping cat holding Busy Bee. "Oh boy," she sighed. "Okay, c'mon, Gidget."

She tried to slip Busy Bee out of the big cat's grasp without waking him up, but the cat sunk his claws into Busy Bee. Gidget tried to pull Busy Bee loose. *SQUEAK!* The huge cat woke up with a roar! "MUROOWWWRR!"

Gidget grabbed Busy Bee and ran around the top of the tower. "Norman, now!" she shouted.

"You got it, sister!" Norman said from the vent where he was watching everything. He used a laser pointer to aim a red dot of light next to Gidget. The big cat's eyes widened. He chased the red dot, trying to catch it. Norman shined the red dot on the floor. The gigantic cat dove off the tower, landing on the floor with a loud *THUD!* Other cats surrounded the mega-cat. They all looked up at the tower, which was wobbling from the big feline's jump. *WOBBLE, WOBBLE, WOBBLE!*

At the top of the rocking tower, Gidget tried to hold on, but that meant dropping Max's beloved stuffed toy. "Busy Bee!" Gidget cried as it rolled and fell off the tower, landing on the floor below. The cats on the floor looked up at Gidget and started to climb the tower to get at her!

"Okay," Gidget said. "Time for plan B!"

"Engaging plan B!" Norman responded.

The guinea pig pointed the laser's red dot on the tower next to Gidget, where all the cats down below could see it. Gidget reached out her paw, pretending to cover the dot. Norman switched off the laser so it looked like the dot was under Gidget's paw. Gidget closed her paw and lifted it up for everyone to see. Then she opened her paw and Norman hit it with the laser. It looked as though Gidget were holding

Max and **Duke's** life change dramatically when their owners have a baby. New York City is a big and scary place, making overprotective Max a little anxious trying to keep the little tike away from . . . well . . . **everything**.

When **Gidget** loses Max's favorite toy, she's forced to do something no dog has ever done before: **go undercover as a cat!**

The only way to really be a cat is to be born a cat—
but **Chloe's** intense training gets Gidget as close
as any dog has ever come.

Snowball is a mild-mannered bunny by day, eating cereal and playing video games with his little girl, but at night, he becomes . . .

CAPTAIN SNOWBALL!

When crime calls, he answers with his two furry fists of fury, **Paw & Order**.

Mel and **Buddy** are always willing to help their friends, no matter how wild the adventures get.

Pops was just trying to teach his owner's new puppy
the ropes of being a dog, but somehow the old dog ended
up having to teach every puppy in the neighborhood.

Pops has taught his students **Princess**, **Pickles**, and **Tiny** that staring at humans with big, round **puppy eyes** is a great way to get what they want.

the red dot in her paw. The cats all gasped!

Finally, Gidget opened her mouth and ate the red dot! Norman switched off the laser so the dot disappeared.

A chubby cat's jaw dropped open in disbelief. "She caught the red dot!"

"HUZZAH!" cheered all the cats.

Gidget leapt off the tower and picked up Busy Bee.

"She is the Chosen One!" a cat announced.

"All hail the Queen!" the huge cat shouted.

"Hail to the Queen!" the cats all cried, bowing down to Gidget.

In a field on the farm, a small herd of steers started a stampede. But before they could get anywhere, Rooster sprinted ahead of them and stared them down. The cattle turned around and headed back to their pen. "Git 'er!" Rooster snapped, nipping at their hooves to keep them in line. "Faster!" The steers quickened their pace.

Max and Duke watched. "Max, did you see

that?" Duke asked, excited.

"Yeah," Max said, unimpressed. He was tired and annoyed from his sleepless night.

"So cool," Duke said admiringly.

Max frowned. "Aww, it's not that big a deal."

Rooster ushered the last few cattle into the pen. "Move! Yah! Move it!" He pushed the metal gate closed with his nose. *CLANG!*

"Oh man," Duke said, super impressed by Rooster.

As Rooster left, a huge pig pushed open a gate and trotted out of his pen into the yard. "Hey, look!" Max said. "That big guy got out!"

"We'd better get Rooster back," Duke said.

Max thought about it, then said, "No. No need for that. I can handle it." He walked up to the pig, who stood still, looking bored. "Hey, mister!" he called to the pig. "Back! Back inside! C'mon!"

The hog looked at Max and turned away. Max looked over at Duke, who nodded. "Yup," Max said. He turned back. The pig was ignoring him. He tried pushing the pig from the side.

"You're doing great!" Duke called. "Go underneath him!"

"Let's go!" Max told the pig.

"I think he moved a little," Duke said.

Max walked around and got in front of the pig, facing him. "Don't you ignore me!" he warned. The pig kept chewing a bunch of radishes. Max yanked the radishes out of the pig's mouth, but the pig just picked up another bunch and started eating them. "Ahh, come on!" Max said. Max jumped onto the pig's back.

"Uh, Max, Rooster nips at the sheep to get 'em to move," Duke suggested.

Max was jumping up and down on the pig's back. "Really?" he said. "That sounds drastic, but okay—pig, you asked for this." He bit the pig's tail.

SQUEAL! The pig bucked Max off his back, sending him flying into a fence. *WHACK!* Max's impact knocked a few boards out of the fence, and sheep filed out of the new gap. Max staggered to his feet.

"Hey, Max," Duke said, concerned. "You okay?"

"Yeeaaah," Max said slowly, feeling dizzy. "How's the pig?"

Duke looked at the pig, who was still standing outside the barn, eating. "He's doing good."

Looking concerned, Rooster ran up. "What's going on?"

"Don't worry," Max assured him. "I'm fine."

"You let all the sheep out!" Rooster said accusingly.

"I did?" Max said, confused.

Rooster ran over to the escaping sheep and barked, "Hey! Get back in there! C'mon!" The sheep obediently turned around and headed back into the pen. "Wait a minute," Rooster said as he studied the flock. "Where's Cotton?"

"Oh, he went into the woods," one of the sheep answered.

Rooster sighed. Then he turned to Max. "You," he said sharply. "Come with me."

"Where are we going?" Max asked.

"We're gonna go get Cotton back," Rooster said firmly.

Max swallowed nervously. But he didn't want Rooster to know he was nervous, so he just said, "Oh, great." He turned to his brother and said, "Come on, Duke."

"Duke, sit," Rooster commanded.

Duke sat, saying, "Yup."

The farm dog told Max firmly, "This is just you and me."

"Oh boy," Max said, not doing a very good job of pretending to be excited.

"Come on," Rooster said, heading toward the woods.

Max followed him, saying, "Oh, super." He looked back at Duke.

"Goodbye!" Duke said.

Max walked toward the dark, scary woods with Rooster.

Rooster was bounding through the woods, making it look easy. "Cotton!" he called. "Where are you?"

Max was finding it much tougher to run through the forest. He had to dodge limbs and sticks and weeds and rocks. It was nothing like strolling down a New York City sidewalk. Brambles caught in his fur, and branches smacked him in the face. *WHACK!*

Rooster looked back at Max, who was struggling to keep up. "Come on!" he yelled. "Hurry up!"

They crossed a stream. Rooster leapt from rock to rock, arriving at the opposite bank completely dry.

Max followed as best as he could. Ahead, Rooster was easily jumping over bushes full of thorns.

Max stopped when he reached the bushes and stared at all the thorns, pretty sure he couldn't jump over them. "Come on!" Rooster urged. "Just jump!"

Max lowered himself and then sprang into the air . . . and right into the bushes. "Ow! Ow! Ow! Ow!" he cried as he pulled himself out of the tangle of sticker-bushes.

"Scent's getting stronger," Rooster told him. "Cotton's close." He started climbing up a steep hill.

Max looked up the slope. "Oh boy." He tried to follow Rooster, talking himself through the difficult climb. "Okay, I can do this. I got it. I got it. . . ." Suddenly, he slipped and slid all the way back down to the bottom of the hill, yelling, "AAHHHHH!"

He tried again, carefully spotting the best places to put his paws. When he finally reached the top, he felt wiped out. Rooster walked on, but Max didn't follow him. "Rooster, you know what?" he said. "Just go on without me. I'm holding you back."

"Oh, you're not giving up, Max," Rooster declared.

"Yeah, but—"

"BAAAA!"

It was Cotton! He had to be nearby! "Follow me!" Rooster said, running off. Max ran after him. Soon they reached the edge of a huge cliff. Peering over the side, they saw a sheep with his hoof caught in the branches of a tree that was growing out of the cliff. The sheep had a goofy smile on his face.

"Cotton, what are you doing down there?" Rooster demanded.

"There are apples in this tree!" Cotton explained cheerfully, if a little dopily.

Rooster studied the rocky cliff between the top edge and the tree below. "All right," he reassured Cotton. "Just don't panic."

Max had crawled up to the edge of the cliff and was peeking over. It was a long way down. "Oh man," he moaned.

"Max is coming down to save you," Rooster told Cotton calmingly.

"Wait," Max said, his dog eyes popping wide. "What?"

Rooster turned to him and spoke quietly. "That tree can't support my weight. You get down there."

Max peered over the edge again. It looked really dangerous. "I . . . I can't do that," he admitted.

"Sure you can," Rooster said. "Think of this as a game of fetch. Now go fetch the sheep."

Max thought about it, but it still seemed impossible. "No," he said. "No, no, no, no. It's too high, and I'm too afraid."

Rooster drew a little closer to him. "Max, here's a trick. The first step of not being afraid is acting like you're not afraid."

Max looked Rooster in the eye, mulled over what the older dog had said, and nodded.

"So," Rooster asked, "are you scared?"

"No," Max said in a weak, unconvincing voice.

"Are you scared?" Rooster repeated.

"No!" Max said louder. "No, I'm not!"

"Now you're talking!" Rooster said, grinning. "Go get Cotton! Hurry!"

Max looked far down the cliff at Cotton stuck in the tree. Cotton smiled up at him. "Hey," the sheep said in a friendly greeting.

Max took a deep breath. "Okay," he said. He

lowered himself over the edge, cautiously making his way from rock to rock down the cliff. "Listen, Cotton," Max called to the sheep. "Walk toward me, okay?"

"Okay, sure," Cotton agreed. "But my leg is stuck." He showed Max how his leg was caught in the tree's branches.

Max called up to Rooster, "His leg is stuck!"

"Well, unstuck it!" Rooster called down to him.

"Uh," Max said, unsure how to do that. He carefully started edging out onto the trunk of the sideways tree. He slipped a little. The tree shifted. . . .

"Hold on!" Rooster warned.

And the tree started to fall!

"Wheeee!" Cotton sang happily, oblivious to the danger.

"YAAAHHHH!" Max screamed as the tree fell. *CRUNCH!*

The tree wedged against the opposite wall of the canyon. It stopped falling . . . for the moment. But Max wasn't sure how securely it was wedged between the two rocky cliffs. "Okay, Cotton, listen," he said. "We gotta—"

The tree started to slip again. "AAAHHH!" Max yelled.

"Hurry up!" Rooster shouted.

Slowly making his way across the tree, Max climbed toward Cotton. He stretched forward and grabbed the sheep by the tail with his mouth. Then, using all his strength, Max wrenched Cotton free of the branches and swung him over to a rocky ledge to relative safety. "Whoa!" Cotton exclaimed. Max jumped onto the ledge just in time. The tree plummeted into the canyon. *WHUMP!* It slammed into the ground far below.

With rocks sliding under his feet, Max pushed Cotton up the wall of the cliff. Finally Cotton made it to the top, but Max lost his grip and started to fall!

"AHHHH!" he screamed.

CLOMP! Rooster leaned way over the edge of the cliff, grabbed Max's collar in his teeth, and yanked the little dog up to safety. Max looked around, tired and bruised. "We're alive!" he gasped, hardly able to believe it.

"Yup!" Rooster confirmed.

"Yeah, we are— OH NO!" Cotton said, almost

falling over the edge. Rooster grabbed him and pulled him away from the canyon. "Yeah, we are!" Cotton repeated cheerfully.

Back near the barn, a few of the sheep saw something coming their way. Duke followed their gaze and saw Max, Rooster, and Cotton coming out of the woods. Max was beat-up, dirty, and extremely proud. "Max!" Duke called to his brother.

"Get back in your pen, Cotton," Rooster ordered.

"Okay!" Cotton agreed, always chipper. He headed back toward the woods.

"Other way, Cotton," Rooster told him.

"Okay!" Cotton said, turning around and heading into the pen with his fellow sheep.

Duke trotted up to Max. "So how'd it go? What happened?"

"You know, it was pretty intense," Max began. "Tell 'em, Rooster!"

"You know . . . some stuff happened . . . and now it's over," Rooster said dryly as he walked away.

"Wow! He can really tell a story," Duke said

with his usual enthusiasm.

"Right?" Max replied, not sure of what to make of the old farm dog.

In another part of the city, Sergei's wolves entered a dog park. The area was surrounded by skyscrapers, and lights twinkled high in the inky black darkness of the night sky. "We're getting closer," their leader growled as he sniffed the air.

Daisy was holding court with several dogs. "So there I was," she said in a dramatic voice, "surrounded by nasty wolves. Was I scared, you ask?"

"No one asked anything," one dog said. "You just walked up to us and started talking."

Daisy ignored him. "I was scared, but I saved that tiger anyway. Am I a hero? That's not for me to say." She noticed Pepper, a dog with crazy eyes, digging in the dirt. "Pepper! Pepper, are you listening?"

"I am," Pepper answered, still digging.

"Stop digging for a second, Pepper, and maybe

you'll learn something," Daisy said. Just behind her, Sergei's wolves walked up. The other dogs saw them, but Daisy didn't. "As I was saying," Daisy continued, "the moral of the story is 'Believe in yourself.' "

"Wo-wo-wolf!" one of the dogs stammered in fear.

"Duh, that's what I've been talking about," Daisy said, exasperated. "Wolves." But then she noticed the dogs looking past her. She turned around, and the wolves leapt at her! "YIKES!" she yelled. Daisy ran, heading toward the swings.

When the kids on the swings saw her, they said, "Puppy!" But Daisy ran right by them. Disappointed, they said, "Aww!"

The wolves ran up, chasing Daisy. "Doggies!" the kids yelled, excited. But then the wolves snarled and growled. The kids screamed and ran away.

CHAPTER FIFTEEN

Deeper in the park, the wolves looked around, sniffing the air. They spotted a sheepdog walking along through the grass. When the wolves growled at her, the sheepdog stopped in her tracks, whipped around, and ran back the way she had come. She didn't want any trouble with the wolves. Daisy, who had been hiding underneath the shaggy dog, kept walking ahead, unaware that she'd lost her cover. The wolves ran up and surrounded her.

"Where is the tiger?" the lead wolf asked in a slow, menacing voice.

Daisy, with a momentary look of shock on her face as the wolves approached, yelled, "Oh! There he is!"

The wolves' heads snapped around in the direction she indicated. Seeing nothing, they turned around only to find that Daisy had hopped aboard a passing scooter and was already far away.

Snowball was playing an action-packed video game in his living room. He wore his superhero costume with the mask down over his face. On the monitor, a superhero, whom Snowball had made to look as much like him as possible, was fighting other superheroes.

"Ha! Take that!" Snowball barked. "Now, THIS is training, okay? Keeping my reflexes sharp! Ha!" He tossed off his headset. "Oh, you were just beaten by a rabbit, and you don't even know it!"

DING!

"Oh, my pizza rolls!" Snowball said happily.

He hopped toward the kitchen but heard a noise outside. "What's that?" he asked, turning around. He hopped over to the window, opened the blinds, and saw Pops staring in with Hu and the puppies.

"AAHHH!" Snowball screamed, startled. "Oh, it's Pops."

"Hello, Snowball!" Pops called out through the window.

Snowball climbed out onto the fire escape. "Hey, Pops! What's going on?"

"Oh, you know," Pops said. "Just returning your giant tiger. Fun fact: he TRASHED MY APARTMENT! This thing ate a flat-screen TV like it was a pita chip!"

"For shame!" Pickles scolded.

"Uh, are you sure that's my tiger?" Snowball asked, stalling for time. "Because I don't know if that's—"

"Let's go, class," Pops said to the puppies as he turned to leave.

"Come on, old man!" Snowball pleaded. "Don't do this!"

But Pops and the puppies walked away, leaving Snowball alone on the fire escape with Hu. "Hey,"

Snowball said to the tiger, not sure what to do next. "How ya been?"

Hu smiled, happy to see his little bunny pal.

Moments later, Snowball led Hu into Max's empty apartment. Hu immediately started cheerfully chewing on Max's toys. "There you go, Hu!" Snowball told the tiger. The bunny hopped up onto the windowsill, went out onto the fire escape, and closed the window. "Problem solved!"

Across the alley, Gidget looked out the window of her apartment and saw Snowball. She was surrounded by the cats from the old lady's apartment, who now considered her their queen. "Snowball?" she called.

The rabbit looked up. "Puffy Dog?"

"What are you doing in Max's apartment?" Gidget asked.

"Nothing," Snowball lied. "Why are you hanging out with every cat in the universe?"

Loosing Max's favorite toy and having to go undercover seemed way too complicated to explain, so she just said, "Uh, you know, just because."

"Okaaaayyy," Snowball said, not buying it but having to keep cool just the same.

"Okaaaayyy," Gidget said, not believing that Snowball was in Max's apartment for no reason at all. They looked at each other suspiciously.

"Okaaaayyy," Snowball repeated.

CHAPTER SIXTEEN

On the farm, Max trotted through the cool night air, to catch up with Rooster. "Uh, hey, Rooster," he called to the big dog, who was heading toward his special spot on the old truck.

"Hey, kid," Rooster answered. "Good job today."

"Thanks," Max said, smiling. "I gotta admit, I'm feeling pretty good. I'm not so nervous around the farm, or you, or even the turkey." He whipped around and yelled, "YEAH, I SEE YOU, YOU

WEIRDO!" The turkey, who was following him again, froze in its tracks, looking surprised by Max's outburst.

Max continued, "I just heard that we're leaving in the morning, and—"

"AROOOOOO!" Rooster howled as he jumped onto the top of the truck.

"Oh," Max said.

Max watched Rooster howling in the moonlight, unsure of what to do next. "Do you want me to, uh . . . Do you want me to go?" he asked.

Rooster chuckled. "It's just what we do out here. You wanna join me?"

Max was flattered and excited by the farm dog's invitation. "Yeah, okay," he quickly agreed. "Cool!" He hopped up onto the truck.

"You ready to try?" Rooster asked.

Rooster howled again. "AROOOOO!"

Max tried joining in, but he felt shy about it. And his little howl sounded nothing like Rooster's. He howled meekly, "Howroh . . ."

"C'mon, kid," Rooster urged him. "Deeper. Deep. From your gut."

"Right, okay, got it," Max said, hearing the call

of the wild from deep inside him. The two of them howled together. "AROOOOOO!"

"There you go!" Rooster said, smiling.

Max really got into it, letting himself go. It felt good to howl in the night! "AROOOOOO!"

Early the next morning, as Max slept on the front porch of the farmhouse, Rooster dropped a bandanna next to him. Max woke up for a moment, saw the bandanna—just like the one Rooster wore—and said, "Wow." A little awed, he smiled at the bandanna.

Meanwhile, Katie and Chuck packed their luggage into the car. Katie buckled Liam into his seat, and Chuck called the two dogs. "All right," he said. "C'mon, guys."

Duke climbed into the car next to Liam. Max jumped up, wearing the bandanna Rooster had given him. "Huh?" Max said to Duke and Liam, indicating his bandanna. "What do you think?"

"Max!" Liam squealed. "So cool!"

"Hey, where'd Max go?" Duke asked, grinning.

"And who let a supercool cowboy in the car?"

As the car headed down the long driveway, Katie waved to Uncle Shep, calling, "Bye! Thanks for a wonderful visit!"

Uncle Shep waved back. "Goodbye now! So long! Hurry back!"

"Bye, Rooster!" Duke called.

"And thank you!" Max added.

Rooster watched as the car drove into the distance. The big farm dog, usually so tough and calm, actually looked a little bit emotional. Out of the corner of his eye, he watched the turkey, who was staring at him. "Mind your business, turkey," he said. "I'm having a moment."

The turkey got in the old dog's face, peering at him quizzically. Rooster turned. The turkey got in his face again. All the emotion left Rooster's face with a roll of his eye. "Okay, moment's over," he said. He turned back around in a circle and settled down for a quick nap. Shrugging, the turkey lay down and joined him.

That night, tired after the long drive, Katie, Chuck, Liam, and the dogs got home to their apartment in New York City. Chuck carried Liam, who was sleeping, into his bedroom and laid him down on his bed. "There you go, buddy," Chuck said. Katie turned off the lights.

In Liam's bedroom, Duke flopped to the ground. Max lay down on a pillow. "It's good to be home," he said.

"So good," Duke agreed.

They fell asleep.

Snowball tried to sneak past Max without waking him up, but he tripped. "Shush!" he whispered. "Shhh. . . ."

"You shhhhh," Daisy whispered back.

Max opened his eyes just in time to see four big tiger paws walk past. "Huh?" he said, wondering if he was dreaming. "Snowball!"

"Oh, hey," Snowball said, trying to act casual. "Hey, Tiny Dog."

"What are you doing with a tiger in my apartment?" Max demanded.

Snowball thought fast. "Well," he said, "what are YOU doing home from your trip so soon, hmm?

As long as we're pointing fingers."

"We don't have time for this!" Daisy warned. "The circus wolves are closing in! We gotta hide Hu!"

Max's eyes widened. "Circus wolves?"

"You do know I have a life when you're not around," Snowball said. "Right, T.D.?"

"Yeah, okay," Max said. "But—"

Daisy looked out the window. "Captain Snowball!" she hissed. "They're here!"

CHAPTER SEVENTEEN

"Whaaaat?" Snowball hissed back.

He ran to the window. Max followed him. They peered out and saw the wolves creeping up the fire escape. In the alley below, a van was parked with its headlights on. Max watched as Snowball, Daisy, and Hu freaked out. "Wolves!" Snowball cried. "Oh no, no, no, no, no! This is IT! Oh, we're going to die! No!"

"Keep it together, boy," Daisy said.

"Okay, okay," Snowball said, wiping away his sniffles. "We need a plan. Daisy! Let's hide Hu on the roof!" The rabbit noticed Max slowly climbing out the window. "Tiny Dog, where are you going?"

"I'm not sure," Max admitted. "But I guess I'm gonna try to find my inner Rooster."

Snowball tried to figure out what Max was talking about, but he couldn't come up with anything. "What?" he asked, confused.

There was no time to explain. Max bravely headed down the fire escape toward the circus wolves. As two of the wolves came toward him, Max barked at them. "ROWF! ROWF!" Two more wolves surrounded Max, snarling and ready to pounce. He backed up . . . right into Sergei's legs.

Laughing, the cruel circus master kicked Max through an open window, into the basement. "Puny little coward," he sneered.

Max struggled to reach up to the basement window.

Meanwhile, Snowball and Daisy led Hu up the fire escape to the roof. "Hurry up, Hu!" Snowball urged. Once they'd reached the rooftop, Snowball said to Daisy, "All right, let's hide Hu in the—"

But before Snowball could finish, Little Sergei the monkey hopped up onto the roof. "Aaaah!" Snowball yelled, thinking the wolves had arrived. "Oh, it's just this weird little guy," he said, relieved. He faced Little Sergei. "Why don't you just go back to wherever you belong, Bonzo, because I don't want to have to—"

Little Sergei grabbed Snowball by the ears. "Ow," Snowball said. The monkey flipped Snowball back and forth, slamming him against the ground. "OW-OW-OW-OW-OW-OW!" Snowball yelled. Finally, Little Sergei tossed the rabbit into a vent.

At that same moment, the wolves reached the roof. "Run, Hu!" Daisy gasped. She tried to block the wolves from reaching the young tiger, but the beasts just swatted her aside. They cornered Hu just as Sergei arrived with a tranquilizer gun. *THWOCK!* The tranquilizer dart stuck in Hu's side.

Sergei felt something and looked down. Daisy had latched onto his leg, biting his pants and pulling. "Oh, pretty little dog," Sergei said, grinning evilly. "I like you. You will join my circus. As a cannonball!" He reached down and grabbed Daisy. She barked like crazy, but it was no use. The little dog couldn't escape Sergei's grip.

Max finally managed to scramble out of the basement window just in time to see Sergei hand Daisy to a clown, who was standing next to the van in the alley. "Mongrel doesn't learn," Sergei said.

He turned to Hu, caged in the van, as Max watched from behind a garbage can. "Stupid tiger!" Sergei shouted.

Hu, dazed from the tranquilizer and scared at being locked up again, gave Max a look that said, "Please help me" just before Sergei slammed the van's back doors closed.

"Pathetic," he said. "Let's go! We have a train to catch!"

As Sergei climbed in the front and the van took off, Snowball fell out of a vent onto the sidewalk. He ran after the van, yelling, "Daisy! Hu!" But the van was too fast. It left him in the dust. He stopped, out of breath, and turned to Max. "What are we gonna do, T.D.?" he panted.

Max had an idea. He smiled.

Moments later, Max and Snowball were rocketing down the street, holding tight to Norman's remote-control car. Max was on the back of the little car, and Snowball was on the front. "WOO-HOO!" Snowball whooped, enjoying the speed. "WHOOAAA! HA HA!"

As they zoomed by a guy on a motorcycle, Snowball tapped a button on Norman's walkie-talkie. "ATTENTION! This is Captain Snowball!"

In the apartment full of cats, Gidget heard Snowball's voice over the walkie-talkie saying, "Me and Tiny Dog need backup!"

"We read you loud and clear!" Gidget said into her walkie-talkie. "Over!"

". . . to the circus," Snowball's staticky voice explained through the little speaker. ". . . is urgent! Over!"

"Copy that!" Gidget confirmed into her walkie-talkie. She turned to Busy Bee. "Busy Bee," she said, "Mommy's gotta go save Daddy, again." She faced her loyal army of cats. "Cats! Let's do this!"

The cats knew just what to do. They dumped their food in the garbage. Then they took their empty bowls to the sweet, little old lady and showed them to her with big, longing eyes, meowing.

"Are my babies hungry?" the lady asked. With some effort, she got up out of her chair and went to the kitchen. When she opened the cabinets, they were empty. "Ooooh, dear," she sighed. Realizing a trip to the store was in order, the old lady popped in her hearing aids and dentures and grabbed her purse and keys.

Moments later, she was barreling down the street in her great big old car with Gidget and all the cats. "Buckle up, everyone!" she called.

"Hang on, Max!" Gidget said into her walkie-talkie. "We're coming!" She told the cats, "Floor it!" They pressed down on the gas pedal and took control of the steering wheel.

"Ooooooh!" the old lady cooed.

The car raced through the brightly lit streets of New York City.

CHAPTER EIGHTEEN

At a railyard near Coney Island, clowns were packing up Sergei's circus and loading it onto train cars. Yanking Hu behind him on a chain, Sergei barked, "Hurry up, you clowns!"

Hu tried to pull free, but Sergei kept a firm grasp on the chain. "Let's go!" he snarled. "Let's go!" Sergei pulled the tiger into the engine car at the front of the train. He attached the chain to a metal bar, declaring, "You will not escape from Sergei!"

The engineer was ready to drive the train. "All right," Sergei told him, "let's get this show on the tracks!" The engineer pulled a lever, and the train started chugging away from the station.

Norman, Snowball, and Max raced into the railyard on the turbo-charged remote-control car. "WHOAAA! HA HA HA HA!" Snowball whooped.

They jumped the tracks. Max and Snowball leapt off the car and flew through the air toward the train. *WHAM!* Norman landed hard. He was okay, but the car fell apart.

Max reached the train's caboose and climbed onboard. "Snowball!" he shouted back. "Come on! Jump!"

As the train sped up, Snowball leapt toward it. He fell just short of the caboose, but Max caught his ears and hauled him in.

Inside the old lady's car, Gidget spoke into her walkie-talkie. "Guys, what's your location?"

Still holding his tiny steering wheel, Norman pressed the button on his walkie-talkie and answered, "They're on a train headed north. Over!"

"Roger that, Norman!" Gidget responded. "We're on it!" She lowered her walkie-talkie and told the cats on the steering wheel, "Turn right here!"

SCREECH! As the cats yanked the wheel, the car made a sharp turn to the right and exited the highway.

As the circus train sped through the night, Max and Snowball ran along the top of the train cars. Snowball burst ahead, doing his best superhero rolls and somersaults.

"You hang back, T.D.!" he called. "Captain Snowball is on the caaaaaaaaaase!" As he said *case,* Snowball fell through a skylight into one of the cars.

"Snowball!" Max cried.

"I'm fine!" Snowball reassured him from the train car.

Max peered down through the skylight. "Can you find a way to get back up here?"

Before Snowball answered, Max heard growling.

He turned around and found himself face to face with four circus wolves!

"AAAAAHHHH!" he screamed as he ran away. Tiny Max zipped under a pole that hung over the passing train. Three of the wolves saw the move and ducked. The fourth wolf was not so lucky— WHACK! Unconcerned about their companion falling from the train, the remaining wolves continued to chase Max.

From below, Snowball saw the wolves leap over the open skylight. "Tiny Dog!" he yelled. But Max was gone. Snowball looked around the train car he'd fallen into. "Hello?" he called when he heard a noise in the shadows. "HELLO?"

He passed by a stack of boxes, and then he saw Daisy! She was loaded into a cannon that was aimed into the air!

"Daisy!" Snowball cried, thrilled to see her.

"Oh, thank goodness!" she said, equally thrilled to see Captain Snowball.

Suddenly, the train car flooded with light. Little Sergei wheeled into the room on a unicycle. He juggled a few bowling pins menacingly. He threw one at Captain Snowball, but the bunny ducked.

Fury welled up in the rabbit as he leapt into action. He and Little Sergei bounced around the room as the rabbit unleashed a flurry of martial arts moves against the bad monkey.

"This ends NOW, monkey!" Snowball said, blocking another pin. Then something occurred to Snowball that delighted him. "Oh! You're a supervillain! You are my ARCHENEMY!"

BAM! A bowling pin hit Captain Snowball and knocked him out cold.

Up on top of the train cars, the growling wolves were still chasing Max. Once again, Max slid to the side of the train to avoid an upcoming sign. The wolf right behind Max attempted the same move, but his greater weight sent him sliding off the edge.

"Two down. Two to go," Max thought as he scrambled to stay ahead of his pursuers.

The next train car carried a full load of pipes stacked high. Max's back leg kicked a tie loose, causing some of the pipes to slide free. Getting an idea, Max poured on the speed and reached the other side of the train car. He bit through the other tie, releasing the pipes completely.

The pipes rolled from under the paws of the wolves. Before the wolves could reach their prey, they tumbled off the train and into the night.

Max breathed a sigh of relief. Then he raced off to find his friends.

CHAPTER NINETEEN

As Captain Snowball opened his blurry eyes, he saw Little Sergei coming toward him. The monkey had lit the bowling pins on fire and was juggling the flaming weapons. He chased Snowball around the cannon. Smiling wickedly as he rode by the fuse, the monkey backed up and lit it with one of the pins.

Daisy's eyes went wide at the sight of the sparkling fuse. "Um, Captain Snowball . . . ," she said, trying to alert him.

"Oh no!" Snowball ran up to the cannon, looking for a way to put the sparkling fuse out. Little Sergei charged at Snowball from behind and slammed into the fuzzy hero. The force knocked Snowball into the side of the cannon, causing it to tip over. As the two adversaries continued to fight, the cannon slowly settled into a position level with the ground. Now that it wasn't pointed upward, Daisy was able to crawl out.

Seeing that his friend was free, Snowball turned to concentrate on Little Sergei. The mean little monkey was going to get it now. Little Sergei spun around to take on Snowball, but Daisy rotated the cannon, separating the two quarreling creatures. The cannon forced Little Sergei her way, and when he got to Daisy, she was waiting. She pushed the monkey right into his own trap.

Little Sergei shrieked when he realized the fuse was still lit.

BOOOOOM!

Running across the top of the train, Max looked up to see Little Sergei soaring through the air like a shooting star. His mouth dropped open in disbelief—that shooting star was shooting straight at him!

WHAM!

Max was sent flying off the train.

Max scrambled to his feet and scanned the landscape. The engine was pretty far away, but it was down a hill and rounding a curve. Max realized that he just might be able to catch up with it before it reached the tunnel in the distance.

"I can head them off!" he said determinedly. Running as fast as he could, Max bounded down the hill and through the woods, heading toward the train tracks.

Max ran as fast as his four legs could carry him. He got to the top of the tunnel just as the train was about to enter it. Without even thinking about the consequences, Max took a deep breath and leapt into the air . . .

CRASH!

Max shattered a window as he smashed into the train. He landed on his feet in front of Sergei. The man still held Hu on a chain. Max looked up and growled at the evil circus owner.

"All right, doggy. Bring it o— YEE-OWW!" Sergei didn't finish his sentence because Max had just bit him on the butt!

At that moment, Daisy and Snowball arrived and joined the fight. Sergei had little room to move as he was attacked by the creatures from all sides. Inspired by his friends' bravery, Hu pounced. The tiger tackled Sergei to the ground.

With that, the train engineer pulled the brake. *SCREEECH!*

Everyone went flying out of the train engine.

Outside on the ground, the animals and Sergei struggled to their feet. The animals quickly took the opportunity to get away, but just as they started to leave, Hu was jerked back on his chain.

Sergei glared at them. He was covered in dirt and his clothes were ripped, but he held the chain tightly.

"STOP! You are going NOWHERE!" the cruel man said. "I've had enough!" He laughed, thinking he finally had the animals where he wanted them. Sergei pulled out a gun. The animals froze. Sergei cocked the gun, ready to shoot. "This ends HERE and N—"

WHAM! The cat lady's big car slammed right into Sergei, sending him tumbling through the air! "WAAAAAH!" he screamed.

Loud music poured out of the car as it spun around, kicking dust and dirt into the air. Stunned, Sergei struggled to rise through the cloud of dust.

The other animals cheered! Max, Hu, Snowball, and Daisy jumped through the car window.

"Max!" Gidget called.

"Gidget!" he answered.

The cat lady smiled as she adjusted her glasses and turned up the volume on the radio. She put the car in reverse with a solid pull on the gear shift. Sergei staggered as he tried to run, but she slammed into him again as she backed the car up.

The cat lady shifted gears and pushed the gas pedal to the floor. The car's back wheels spun, spewing rocks and dirt into the defeated Sergei's face. Then it sped off into the night.

CHAPTER TWENTY

As the sun came up over New York City the next morning, pets woke up and started their days. When Chloe tried to wake her owner up, her new friend Hu helped out. First he jumped onto the bed. Then he tried softly patting the owner's face with his big paw. But she just kept sleeping.

Hu looked at Chloe. She nodded.

"ROWWWRRRR!" Hu roared. The owner leapt up onto the bed's headboard.

By her owner's reaction, Chloe knew that Hu wouldn't be able to stay with her. She wondered for a long time where a large, friendly jungle cat could go live happily ever after. She smiled as the answer came to her.

When Hu and Chloe cautiously entered the cat lady's apartment, they were ready to hear a scream. But when the cat lady set her bespectacled eyes on Hu, it was love at first sight. She beckoned him over to her with glee, and Hu leapt into her arms, causing the old lady to fall over laughing.

In Snowball's apartment, Molly woke up her pet bunny. He was exhausted from his adventures saving Hu. Molly set Snowball in front of a mirror and took off his superhero outfit. Then she dressed him in a new costume. He sleepily opened his eyes and looked in the mirror. "AAAAH!" he screamed.

He was dressed as a pretty princess.

"Hey, man, what is going on?" he asked. Then he turned to one side and the other, checking himself out. "This is . . . AWESOME! Wow!"

Later that morning, Max walked out of his apartment building with Katie, Chuck, Liam, and Duke. "Come on, buddy!" Katie said.

"This is gonna be fun!" Chuck added.

"Woo-hoo!" Liam cheered.

As they walked down the sidewalk, Max thought, "Everything changes. Nothing stays the same for long. The minute you're used to something—the minute you think, 'Oh, this is how life is'—life finds a way of surprising you. You never know what life is going to throw at you, and you have two choices. Run from it, or run at it."

They arrived at Liam's new preschool. "It's a big day," Max thought. "From this point on, nothing is going to be the same."

Liam looked up at the school with big eyes. "Wow."

"But I'm gonna be brave," Max told himself. "And I'm gonna help Liam be brave." He gave Liam a little lick and gently nudged him forward, into the preschool's playground. "Because Liam's my kid," Max thought, "and I want him to see the world. The big, scary, INCREDIBLE world."

Liam ran into the playground to join the other kids.

Duke turned to Max. "Are you okay?"

Max thought about it. "Yeah, I'm good."

As they turned to go home, they heard Liam call, "Wait!"

They turned back, and Liam ran up to them. Hugging Max and Duke, he said, "My doggies."

"Always," Max thought with a smile.